Maurice Leitch

THE HANDS OF CHERYL BOYD

AND OTHER STORIES

Maurice Leitch

THE HANDS OF CHERYL BOYD
AND OTHER STORIES

Hutchinson
London Melbourne Auckland Johannesburg

This edition first published in 1987 by Hutchinson,
an imprint of Century Hutchinson Ltd, Brookmount House,
62–65 Chandos Place, London WC2N 4NW

Century Hutchinson Australia Pty Ltd
PO Box 496, 16–22 Church Street, Hawthorn,
Victoria 3122, Australia

Century Hutchinson New Zealand Ltd
PO Box 40-086, Glenfield, Auckland 10,
New Zealand

Century Hutchinson South Africa (Pty) Ltd,
PO Box 337, Bergvlei, 2012 South Africa

British Library Cataloguing in Publication Data

Leitch, Maurice
    The Hands of Cheryl Boyd : and other stories.
    I. Title
    823'.914 [F]   PR6062.E/

                ISBN 0-09-172632-8

Printed and bound in Great Britain

Contents

Black Is The Colour

When his friend first broached the idea of the outing to him they were in a bar, downtown, late on Saturday afternoon, that period just after the football matches have ended and an hour of intense pint drinking still remains before the pubs empty at tea-time in readiness for the hard night ahead.

'Here we have a situation full of infinite potential,' his red-haired friend had said. 'Coloured crumpet, *bored* coloured crumpet, mark you, stranded here in this God-forsaken hole for one whole day and night, and all we have to do to avail ourselves of what is on a plate is offer ourselves as escorts.'

A deep suck at the brown beer and already warm personal thoughts of skin, teeth, kinky hair.

'But I can see that the idea might well appeal to you,' laughed his friend, noted lecher and expert on women. 'You haven't forgotten my own little experience that time in the big smoke, have you? No, I can see that you haven't.'

But Cindy, 'Large Tan Chest For Sale', indolently lounging in baby-doll pyjamas in a Queensway basement flat, whom his friend had so enthused about, was only one of the many coffee-coloured images that came and went in his head over the next twenty-four hours. And, as the time drew nearer to that appointment outside the hostel where the clutch of dusky beauties was staying in his city, imagination quickened thrillingly with the possibilities ahead.

On Sunday morning his friend rang to say he couldn't make it; his wife was acting up again with one of her regular and hysterical demands to see her mother in the country that on this occasion could not be ignored. He had his future as a womaniser to think of and must at all costs keep his own activities on the home-front above reproach. Anyway, couldn't he always go along on his own and do his level hospitable best to keep their little black sisters happy and smiling and, of course, tell him all about it afterwards, ha, ha. He rang off still laughing.

The hostel was a solid, sandstone building in the heart of the city, a bastion of respectability. Plain Presbyterian virgins from the country lodged there; the food was plentiful and filling; no men were allowed on the stairs leading to the young ladies' quarters; and the gates closed promptly at eleven: no harm could come to innocents there. He sat outside in his car, waiting, the radio playing softly. Sunday boredom, his own Northern city's peculiar variety, gnawed gently at him, and the carefully dressed people passing to and from their churches only strengthened his feeling of being an alien on this one day of the week.

Parked there, he cursed his friend, and himself most of all, for landing him in this situation. Was there still time to ease out from the kerb, he wondered, and forget all those fantasies which his imagination had promised and which he now knew so well could not deliver? There was, but still he held back just a little longer. Something deep, some old discontent with always being on the outside of all those vivid exploits of his laughing red-haired friend held him there. Through his windscreen and in the mirror he continued to study the other cars waiting like his own outside the fudge-coloured building. Other men like himself do-gooding for one afternoon, extending the hand of friendship to a brown one. With the same motives? He thought not. Then he saw a movement on the steps and the drivers' doors began to swing outwards into the sunny street.

Switching off the radio he joined the row of men standing there like patient chauffeurs, watching above the roofs of their cars the coloured faces which bobbed now like corks between the portals. Two things struck him instantly: one, there were *men* in the party, far outnumbering the women, in fact; and two, their clothing. Those drab waterproofs, the umbrellas – some of the women had even covered their dark round heads with transparent plastic hoods – made him realise that his half-formed expectation must have been for saris and jungle cottons swirling out into the sober dullness of the Sabbath streets. Now he should really go, he told himself, now, but it was as if he were in the grip of something he must see through to the end.

Down the steps towards them, arms outstretched, tripped that expected figure, plumpish, in her fifties, with a shadowy, background husband somewhere rich enough to dress her as he did and allow her charitable mania full rein. He found himself, eyes fixed on the points of her crocodile-skin shoes, trying unsuccessfully to insert his single murmured sentence, 'Mr O'Brien asked me to come in his place,' into her flow of thanks to all of them, on behalf of their coloured friends, the British Council and herself.

Swiftly she began hustling bent figures through the open car doors. He found himself with a large smiling African in a trench coat sitting on his left and a look in the mirror confirmed that in the back seat was a spinsterish West Indian (he guessed) flanked by two ageless gentlemen with eyes like chocolate drops.

The journey to the Folk Museum was painful. He kept off the vagaries of Irish weather for as long as he could, but finally gave in. The man at his side had said nothing, a gleam of impossibly white teeth his only contribution; the two tiny Malaysians were self-contained and witty with silvery bursts of merriment that crinkled their eyes, and the schoolteacher from Trinidad had a gruff voice that startled him every time she spoke. He had just mentioned the changeableness of the climate for the hundredth time, it seemed, when the rain did come on and they turned in through the Museum gates with the windscreen melting.

'Thatching is still carried on in the remoter areas of the Province, but it is a dying art; just a few old men left to carry on the tradition. It is more economical now to roof with slate or corrugated iron. These photographs show some classic examples of Irish thatching. Perhaps some of you may be able to pick out similarities with your own native styles.'

The guide's voice delicately threaded its way through sensitive areas, but with malice (it was a game for him now) he noted how the word 'native' constituted yet another mine that exploded in the man's mouth. The fair eyelashes fluttered almost imperceptibly with refined pain, then the tall young graduate raced on with his exposition.

The party, too, moved on while he remained before a complex tangle of dusty wood and blackened iron, not bothering to stoop to read the card and its dense print. A short man in black astrakhan headgear was still studying the photographs.

'Don't you find all this very boring, all this useless information?' he whispered, sensing a fellow dissident.

The Middle Eastern visitor smiled engagingly. 'On the contrary,' he said, 'I find your traditions immensely absorbing. In my country we have a vast problem with primitive farming methods. It is only by studying the records of other cultures at a similar stage to our own that we can hope to advance into the twentieth century.' Christ, he thought.

Frozen in a tableau beyond the glass, aproned women on their knees among potato drills stared back at them from the turn of the century; the standing males wore beards and narrow wrinkled suits with the trousers tied below the knee with twine. He passed on, considerably shaken.

Outside the Museum windows the rain roared down, an Irish afternoon's monsoon, and the party of Commonwealth visitors trailed around in their nylon rainproofs peering and poking at the exhibits with pale-palmed hands. He drifted with them now, answering when spoken to, pretending an interest in what they had to say. A few of them made notes and their earnestness depressed him even more. He began to study the few women, more from

10

boredom than anything else, for that carefully hoarded fantasy of tumbling brown limbs and passionate acrobatics had begun to fade, alas, at the first sight of all that rainwear on the hostel steps.

It was her voice that stirred him, deep for a woman, and with an expert anglicisation that, for him at any rate, put her points ahead of any of the other women there, even the two lean young Sri Lankan sisters he'd met earlier. He watched her asking questions of their guide, the brows serious, nodding punctuation into all the facts about churns, creels and the history of local flax. He edged closer.

African, he guessed; a wide face, lowish forehead, a tight helmet of crisp, spiralling hair, the lips strongly negroid exposing pale pink inner glimpses whenever she laughed. Her raincoat, a man's loose one, swung open carelessly, her bare legs looked burnished, and she wore canvas shoes. Her white equivalent would have been schoolmarmish with a slung camera, guidebook and an athletic stride – if it hadn't been for her youth and the laugh.

The laugh. It startled those in the room who heard it for the first time. The others, her travelling companions, merely smiled a little with familiarity. He watched her broad face split and shine, her teeth, gums and eyes disclosing all, innocence and gaiety infecting even the tight-lipped English curator when his careful sentences were riven by her peals. The white men in the company, he noticed, were swaying towards her like plants in a current. One or two hovered around the outskirts of her little group with smiles on their faces that would have enraged their wives.

He withdrew even further into himself. Never one for competition – not that the idea of competing for one of those huge chocolate grins had attained any real itch with him as yet – he merely continued to potter around, threading in and out of the glassed-in exhibits, sighting now and then on his solitary travels framed glimpses of her performance. Once more he cursed his friend and himself, that incurable habit he had of building up future events and sensations to tottering collapse. On the point of slipping out

11

and away unnoticed – the drive was sloping, he could coast straight to the gates without touching the starter – once again he was shunted clear from his intentions by the woman in the crocodile-skin shoes. The next part of the programme, she announced firmly and dramatically, was to be refreshment in the upstairs tearoom, and they followed the direction of her heavily ringed hand. And so the late afternoon dragged out its weary length, into dim evening, in fact, for there was 'so much to see, *so much, still,*' as their hostess frequently put it.

They straggled along after her and the guide over wet gravel, grass and slippery, beaten earth paths to the pride and joy of the folkways department, a cottage deep in the grounds, authentic down to the last detail. Every stone, beam and rafter had been carefully numbered and transported in swaddling for reconstruction from its original site on the Northern coast. They stooped into the low, dark interior, a small oil-lamp with a tin reflector nailed to the whitewashed wall, the only light – he remembered seeing such a lamp in his grandmother's house – and everyone, for the first time that afternoon, came close together with a moulded identity. The guide's voice dropped to an easy conversational level, and his listeners began to glance at one another with a feeling of discovery; he himself looked straight at his negress and when their eyes met he smiled boldly. She smiled back with sufficient warmth, he sensed, to make him feel a quickening in the pit of his stomach and a new resolve that perhaps something could be salvaged from those original fantasies after all.

And from that moment onwards it did seem as though events might sharpen to a pleasurable apex for, after they had all in turn touched and dutifully fingered those domestic bygone realities and smelt the must of turf, cobwebs and old quilts, they were swept off for the last time to 'a little celebration' at the home of Mrs Brownjohn. People even had distinct names now, and not the unremembered ones of the early introductory formalities.

As he drove away from the Museum he grinned to

himself. His passengers sat tight and staid beside and behind him, little dreaming of the new rôles he had manufactured for them, stamping around in swinging monkey-tails over the carpets and beneath the chandeliers of the Brownjohn residence.

He was right about the furnishings of the house, a large cream-painted mansion in the better part of the city, and pleasantly wrong about the 'refreshments' for, there on a marble-topped sideboard, with a mirror to double the delight, was Scotch, Irish, gin, vodka and sherry lined up awaiting them.

After a couple of large whiskies on his feet he went over to 'Hot Chocolate' – he would confide the nickname to her later – and asked point-blank if he could get her something. She was sitting on a low settee with her gleaming knees just far enough apart for him to anticipate possible abandon and she looked up from her talk. 'Um... a dry sherry, please. Yes, thank you,' then turned to the three waiting faces, all white, two male, one female, hovering on a level with her shoulders.

A slight feeling of rebuff nibbled at him as he returned to the sideboard. To show indifference, he took his time about pouring the pale liquid into the tulip-shaped glass, then replenished his own, added ice with the tongs, drank slowly, reflectively, allowing his slow glance to take in the furnishings, watercolours and bric-à-brac of the room, the groups of people sitting or talking, their hostess expertly circulating with a tray of canapés. Eventually he recrossed the room, holding the glasses out in front of him, and sat down on the arm of her settee, sliding himself unobtrusively into the company.

'I played Ophelia in the end-of-term production,' she was saying, 'and after the initial shock no one thought a thing about it. I mean the theatre today's like that, I think. The rules *can* be broken. Of course, Lady Macbeth's the part I really long to play. Like any actress, I suppose.'

She sipped her Tio Pepe, the level dropping by a genteel fraction, and he thought, *what's all this actress crap?* For,

13

like everyone in his part of the world, he lived suspiciously, scenting the bogus in word and gesture.

She continued to talk about the theatre, her deep voice serious now, and he felt an increasing urge to provoke, in some way, one of those magnificent early laughs, but she really was an actress, it seemed; it was her life.

What part of Africa was she from? 'Nigeria,' she said, looking at him.

Very fast he countered with, 'It mustn't be easy to get suitable rôles in London.'

Her home was in Lagos, she was twenty-four, she had taught school, got a scholarship to study in England, lived in a women's hostel now at Finsbury Park in London. He told her about his own childhood in the country, his present teaching job, the staff, his class of nine-year-olds. He didn't tell her about his wife, and he lied about his age. He felt he was talking brilliantly, spinning a web of words out from and around them that sealed both of them off from everyone and everything in the room. His friends told him that he could become quite passionate on such occasions. If only O'Brien could see him now, he thought, appreciate his fine, slow delicacy of approach. What a bulldozer his friend really was when it came to seduction. When he considered it, how many times had he actually witnessed him in one of those glorious sweeping victories he talked so much about, anyway?

A moment later his soul iced over when the party suddenly and unexpectedly began to break up. As if at a signal that had somehow missed him out all the people in the room were rising to their feet and draining their almost empty glasses. His was still almost three-quarters full of neat spirit. The sacrifice was painful but had to be made. He put the untouched tumbler down behind a bowl of gladioli on one of the room's many tiny tables and, with his hidden hand, squeezed the girl's arm above the elbow with just the right amount of intimate conspiracy to ensure that the mood between them would be resumed after this interruption.

In the polite mêlée on the steps outside he had his hand pumped at least half a dozen times. He whispered to her,

'Why don't you come back in *my* car?' They were side by side, smiling and nodding at the hand-shakers. The shadowy lawns of the house in hushed Marlborough Park were now ringing with rich negroid voices. There was a lot of laughter.

'Well?'

Her eyes slid to his, she looked at him in a way she hadn't done before, and he realised his voice must have leaked something of his anxiety. He felt foolish. Then she nodded, and they descended the steps together.

All went well until they got to his car, which he'd parked deliberately last in line on the curving, gravelled driveway in anticipation of an early departure. But self-congratulation turned sour the instant he saw two of his former passengers waiting for him with ready smiles on their faces. The schoolteacher from Trinidad stood with her arm held affectionately by one of the little Malays. She had removed her gold-framed spectacles and white gloves and swung her handbag carelessly. Her escort, who barely reached her shoulder, looked up at his companion with pride. The woman waved and giggled when they got closer and he wanted to fell her where she stood, tumbling her and her man friend into the heavy shrubbery. He had a surrealistic flash of presentiment, a scene translating itself vividly; both of them going over backwards before his two-handed shove, two sets of thin tan ankles poking out from beneath the laburnum, his own wild laughter testifying to it being an Irish joke. When, of course, it wasn't.

Depressed, he drove in silence through the tree-lined avenues between the high, carefully barbered hedges of the rich. In the back seat the little man from the East was flirting with refined courtliness, his whispered compliments drawing guffaws from his new ladyfriend. Her perfume was heavy, filling the car with a scent like crushed lilies. Once or twice he glanced sideways and a smile greeted him, warmer if anything, but he felt sunk in his own despondency. Tomorrow he would have forgotten about her, or nearly, he thought, nearly...

15

They arrived at the hostel and he stopped the car engine. He couldn't think of a thing to say and, for a moment, there was a silence only broken by smothered giggles and a rustling from the back seat. With an effort of will he made his eyes bypass the mirror, made them meet hers. A smile, then, 'Well, I guess –' he began; a raw bellow bursting from the rear and the sound of pulling away followed by whispered pleas, then the schoolteacher was out on the pavement still laughing at the little man and his passionate antics. *Bloody females*, he thought, and the next moment a cool hand squeezed his own and before he could look down at the match they made on the leather seat she was gone, too, out into the city night, both of them waving goodbyes from the step.

Driving his little Malay back to his own lodging in another part of town he certainly didn't feel like encouraging any conversation. But within yards of their drawing away from the hostel steps two elbows came delicately down on top of the seat at his side and before the first set of lights he already felt like a tired taxi-driver with an unwanted and talkative fare.

He was entrusted with the fact that the West Indian schoolteacher's hair was like wild blowing grasses, her skin soft as nightfall, her teeth purest ivory, her eyes, mouth, ears... He hoped he might hurry through the inventory to more intimate parts, at least, but it seemed their short but intense relationship was destined to be a chaste one. The little man sighed deeply, regretfully. He was to be parted, it seemed, from his beloved the following morning. The statement seemed to snag the smooth flow. 'What do you mean?' he said.

The little man sighed again and his fine fingers moved against the dark upholstery.

'One half of our party is to be staying here for three days more. The remaining number fly over the seas to London. Alas, I am London-bound. I may never see my Miss Millicent again.'

He heard himself express sympathy, and with such a measure of sincerity in his voice that he surprised himself.

But then falling silent, he drove like that the rest of the way to his passenger's dropping-off point. They shook hands through the open car window and that was that. On his own drive homewards he kept his thoughts controlled as if it would be dangerous to do otherwise.

At ten-thirty the following morning he rang the hostel. It was morning break and he was standing in the school staffroom, head and shoulders buried in the semi-darkness of the phone shelter. According to the printed directions on the wall an inch away you were supposed to have complete privacy. But his rump felt unprotected and vulnerable to the gaze of all the other teachers in the room. He was certain also they could translate the gist of what he was saying by concentrating, if they wished, on this exposed part of his anatomy. Accordingly, when the phone was lifted at the other end of the line and a brusque female voice demanded, 'Yes?' his face prickled with sweat in the stuffy gloom and he realised to his horror that he couldn't remember his girl's surname. He breathed deeply in concentration until the voice snapped, 'Hello! Hello!'

'Hello,' he said. 'I'm trying to contact someone who is staying at your hostel. She's one of the overseas party. Her name's Miss Leah –'

He coughed at the crucial moment, hoping that the female warder (she certainly sounded like one) would take him up without any more fumbling on his part. Silence followed for such a long time that he was on the point of putting the phone down, relieved in a way that now, at least, his mind would be at rest for hadn't he tried anyway, when a voice said, 'Yes?'

The tone was even more thrilling at a distance, then he was propelled into speech and for a moment chatted deftly about minor matters, just long enough before getting to the real substance of his call. Her hesitation was minimal this time. Yes, she would love to have dinner that evening, about seven-thirty would suit her, at the hostel, seven-thirty, she would see him then. Goodbye...

*

17

Once more he was waiting in his parked car, but now with the busy night traffic sweeping past. He studied himself in the mirror. His shaving had been careful, his use of lotion discreet. An uneasy moment had occurred when his wife had caught a glimpse of him in his finery about to leave the house. She had looked at him steadily through the rising smoke of her cigarette but he'd got out fast, calling over his shoulder that he wouldn't be too late, these Old Boys' reunion dinners were always bloody boring affairs anyway.

And so now here he was one step closer, it seemed, to the fulfilment of all those extravagant lusts which had risen in him again since the morning phone call. Yes, success was almost in sight, he told himself.

Then she came running down the steps, smiling, and he leaned across to open the door for her.

They drove off. She was wearing a soft cotton dress sprigged with tiny blue flowers with some lacy stuff at the neck and on the short sleeves. Her only jewellery was a fine necklace of gold theatrical masks. On the seat beside him there sat a virginal young girl, prim as on her first date, small mesh purse held daintily in white gloved hands.

The hotel where he had booked a table was something of a risk, but then he liked the food and the atmosphere and, anyway, hadn't he chosen the most conspicuous partner possible? Sitting in the upstairs bar over the first drinks his eyes tended to drift to the door each time a newcomer arrived, but then gradually he relaxed into a state of mild recklessness. She was again drinking dry sherry and, associating this with a number of other things he had observed, he put her down as having a tendency towards correctness, like a schoolgirl trying out her etiquette. At the same time, when she began to talk in that deep authoritative way she had about serious matters, it was hard to reconcile the one with the other. Then once more her eyes would gleam, her lips widen, showing dazzling teeth, and her laugh would ring out wild and unrestrained, and he imagined he could almost feel a hot breath from the great African furnace coming out of that pink open mouth.

18

The meal was good as always and the wine warmed both of them into confidences. He asked her to dance but regretted it the instant he began to propel her about the tiny floor. It wasn't that she was a poor dancer, it was just that she danced differently, *off* the beat instead of on. The other couples thinned out leaving them to it, and his humiliation was complete when she gradually began to move away from him, swaying, to dance on her own, flat-footed, arms swinging. The drummer was grinning, men at the other tables looked on avidly, while he kept his own smile glued in place, an awkward reflection, yards away.

Back at the table she giggled. 'Why are you so conscious of your body?'

He smiled into his glass, more or less returned now to his previous control.

'Let us say,' he said, swirling the Beaune, 'I'm more conscious of *yours*.'

There was silence and he felt he had made a risky move. He kept his eyes lowered. Into vision moved a brown hand. He watched until the index finger reached out and touched his wrist lightly. The white cloth framed and held both hands in strong relief. The phenomenon took on a vivid meaning in his mind that he could not explain. He put it down to the effects of the four whiskies and the half bottle of wine he had drunk. Then she laughed, and he looked up to see the stretching smile, the bright eyes, the teeth. He had made ground.

Driving her back to the hostel, the feeling of achievement still rode with him, even though the night was ludicrously young – that eleven o'clock curfew he had forgotten about. When the car stopped there was no time for talk. A rush of words set a time and place for lunch the following day and as she turned away from him to open the door he slid across the seat. Swiftly he put his hands to the gleaming face and kissed her, a mere touch on those full lips, then, 'Goodnight'. Once more that same look from her, considering still, but no wariness now, none. The car door closed and he drove off fast and recklessly humming to the radio. Oh, what a seducer he was.

Next day was gloriously sunny, the best and bluest weather in weeks. It awoke the daredevil in him again. He lied to his wife across the breakfast table; he lied to his headmaster on the phone minutes later. He didn't think, he didn't have to think about what he was saying. Precaution and consequence were just meaningless words.

Looking his best in a short-sleeved sports shirt, he picked up his coloured chick at noon, whirled around the streets until he found a meter, parked in one fast unbroken reverse, and then sauntered past the shops taking the air. He made jokes, parodying events and personalities of the Sunday they first met, and she laughed and laughed. He would stop and smile at her, in reality he was amused at himself, as she leaned against him shaking, the tears streaking her cheeks. Not a thought for any of his wife's girlfriends who seemed to spend their lunch hour racing through the streets in search of nylons and cosmetics and who might see and report back.

They stopped at a souvenir shop to look at the array of tweed and Connemara marble. He held back a mocking comment when he saw she was serious about buying something to take back for a friend in London. She had no taste, that was plain, but it was just as well, he thought, because past experience had taught him that a superior style of dress, looks or accent in a woman tended to sidetrack his basic drives. He was sentimental and a snob but he knew he was and when you admitted your shortcomings to yourself then they veered more towards virtues. Wasn't that right?

Inside the shop he drifted about on his own while she talked to the assistant about the merits of a dull, greenish ashtray. Casually the idea came to him that he would buy something for her, but what? He picked up a small stuffed toy from a shelf and quickly handed it to one of the other shop assistants. His money changed hands and by the time the transaction was completed and the shapeless purchase in his pocket she was coming towards him, smiling broadly. He would keep his surprise for later. It might even provide a double function, pivoting him even faster forwards towards his goal when the time was ripe. He now enjoyed thinking of it in those terms, of plot and countermove, a new rôle for him certainly, but, by God, how easily he had taken to it.

Outside in the hot glare he headed towards a delicatessen because his next surprise was to be a picnic lunch by the sea, only a matter of a half-hour's drive away. They bought salami, cheese, anchovies, French bread, wine, and he allowed her to bully him gently away from more expensive delicacies. He watched benevolently as she supervised the shopping, enjoying the situation as she inspected, smelt and tasted.

The car spun them out of the city and it seemed as though news had gone ahead to sweep a path before them, so fast was the transition from baking pavements to the lush green of the country. His instinct was sure today; he knew a place, the *only* place, by the sea where they would be alone and he enjoyed her bewilderment when finally they turned in through a gateway and bumped over ruts deeper and deeper into what only looked like the heart of the countryside. They were trespassing but he didn't tell her that. He had discovered the lane and its secret a summer ago and had filed it away in his memory for some future use. No idea for what at the time, just a vague feeling to do with assignation, but now that it had proved its value he felt pleased with himself.

A few minutes later she cried out in delight as the car broke through the trees and into the sunlight. The sea rolled and sucked around the legs of an old pier fifty yards away like lazy blue jelly. The grass between had that cropped, billiard-table nap that could only mean that sheep grazed there all year round. Thoughts of a herdsman made him park the car behind some ancient walls, then they walked together over the firm turf down to the edge carrying the bags of food between them.

He wedged a bottle of wine between two submerged rocks in the shadow of the jetty while she made a little encampment and then strolled back to her wiping the drops from his hands.

'Well?' he said.

21

A drip of water fell on to her bare brown neck. She was bent over the rug stretching its plaid patterns flat on the grass.

'Oh,' she cried, laughing, and rubbing her nape,'this is a *lovely* place! The sea, the grass – oh, the sun. I love the sun, don't you?'

With eyes closed and lips spread in a widening smile she fell backwards on to the warm wool, her bare arms and legs stretching lazily outwards. He stood looking down at her, thinking suddenly of a human brown starfish, a sly Gauguin beauty.

Later when he felt more controlled he suggested they should eat. Through half-closed eyes he watched as she buttered the bread. Her fingers gleamed with the oil from the anchovies. The pleasure of being tended. They drank wine from paper cups and both laughed at his appetite as she sliced off more and more of the bread until the baton dwindled and he lay back in the sun with a sigh of contentment.

'I wish I'd brought a pair of trunks,' he said. They were lying side by side.

'Why not go in, anyway?' she said after a pause, her voice lazy, expressionless.

He lay thinking. Then, loudly, he said, 'I think I will, in that case,' and began unbuttoning his shirt. Rapidly he stripped to his underpants and lay for a moment watching her intently for the smallest sign of embarrassment. The sun prickled his legs, the grass felt like sisal beneath his bare back, her closed lids gleamed while her lips still held that wide cat-like grin of contentment. He stood up and his shadow fell full across her face. She would have to open her eyes now. The happy brown mask showed no change, the human starfish merely stirred sensuously below him seeking the sun. He ran to the water and plunged in.

Soon the cold shock and the threshing about had altered his mood and he shouted to her to come and join him. He saw her sit up on the rug.

'The water's lovely!' he called, blowing out spray.

22

Then she began to unbutton her blouse and he felt a shake of excitement. Now there was a tiny chattering of the teeth as well, and all the time she was looking straight at him, still smiling, her fingers slower at their task, it seemed to him, than was normal. He watched as the blouse came off to disclose a dazzling white brassière, his eyes smarting at the sharp perfection of those moulded cups and straps, light on dark, rare and unexpected as a photo's negative. He became conscious of the stillness, the soft slap of the waves, the sigh of distant foliage, but most of all of the tableau they formed, himself up to his waist in the water and her out there on the rug facing him, and something unseen and electric between.

Then she let herself fall slowly back on to the rug and a great yell of delight burst from him. The idea of her *sunbathing!* He kicked up explosions of foam, the water glinting like chandeliers, then he wallowed and splashed until there was a roaring in his ears and he had to crouch in the shallows breathless and blinded, his face streaming.

When he opened his eyes she was standing facing him shyly a few yards away up to her ankles in the white water. He looked at her, then rose and took her by the hands. Tenderly he towed her out – he felt painfully protective for some reason, engineering the rising level on that chocolate skin an inch at a time as if fearing a hiss if he were careless. She gasped but went with him at his speed. In a moment they were romping and laughing together, partners in a game, an innocent game, despite what he could see now more clearly as the water soaked her cotton to transparency.

Later, when they were lying side by side drying in the sun, he felt desire return. He turned his head sideways. Brown skin patterned with shining globules of sea water which wobbled, broke, then ran in streaks. A shift of position, sly and silent on the warm rug, brought further perspective. A cupped breast, mountainous, rising to firmness, its dark tipped disc outlined clearly through the wet fabric, then lower, the mound, a few escaping hairs, fine wiry coils on the smooth inner thigh.

As he lay there, palms open to the sun, he thought of

something beyond the closeness of the body by his side. No motive made him get up carefully, walk across the grass to where his trousers lay, slide a hand into a pocket; it was just something that entered his mind like a stone falling into a pond.

'Here,' he said, when he got back to the rug. She opened her eyes, squinting up at his dark bulk – the sun was immediately behind him.

'It's for you,' he said. 'A souvenir of Ireland.'

She took the toy from him still uncomprehending, touching it with a look on her face that he couldn't fit into place. He felt cheated, then mildly alarmed, as she continued running her pale fingertips over the furry hide of the little animal without a word or an upward look now.

Her head was averted, he couldn't see her eyes and any hint they might hold of what was troubling her – he could certainly sense that, at any rate – but then on her cheeks he saw twin rolling tears. *My God*, he thought, and the sun seemed to darken. He touched her bare arm tentatively, then her face came up and he saw the unexpected, a shining look, gratitude, a melting softness.

She kissed him on the mouth and said, 'No one ever gave me anything before.' The words had no meaning for him then. Only later were they to unfold.

He laid his hands on her shoulders – they felt hot – the straps of her brassière cool, bisecting ribbons on his palms, and he returned the kiss, gently at first, then with more insistence. She fell slowly backwards on to the rug and now she began to moan, 'No, no, no,' in a low stream in his ear as he nuzzled her neck. But even he knew from his limited experience that the word had no real strength, was contradicted, in fact, by the returning pressure of body, hands and thighs on his own.

Over a tawny shoulder, strapless now, he stared at the glass-button eyes of the little toy donkey on the rug. Its short legs were straddled inside a green plaid rectangle. The turf in its twin creels had an authentic dusty look. He felt like Gulliver for a moment, then was brought back painfully

24

to reality as fingernails began raking his bare back. A vision of red streaks for his wife to glimpse and interpret galvanised him into a theatrical show of passion. In reality it was an attempt to pin her arms. She began to bite his neck. Frantically he hunched his shoulders and ran his hands down to where he hadn't dared send them before. She yielded to him unreservedly.

Their love-making was brief, intense and savage. He was made conscious of the disparity in the strength of their passions, and it was no use blaming his inadequacy on worry about the darkening bruises on his neck and shoulders. She was wringing him tirelessly, and he knew he was beaten at what should have been his game. But this had turned out to be a different game with a different set of rules...

Afterwards they lay, still joined, a fine film of sweat mixing on their limbs, his face suspended inches away from a small area of bruised grass. He studied the miniature jungle, the tangled growth, insect life, silently and with great concentration.

She began to weep then and sob with painful, racking gasps. Their bodies broke. He looked at her curved back, the pattern of her vertebrae, the globes of her buttocks, across three feet of rug, but the distance might have been miles, an ocean, a continent.

Then she jerked out of her foetal crouch and threw her arms and legs out stiffly, rolling her head back and forth, round and round, in despair. She beat the rug with brown fists making dents that slowly filled as the wool jerked beneath her attack. All he could do, say, was a weakly repeated, 'Please, please.' He was afraid to touch her now, afraid of *her* and this animal grief.

When she was calmer, with only the occasional whimpering shudder, he did touch her – gently. She looked ugly now, her hair coarse and metallic, face puffy and streaked with tear tracks. A weeping fit was something he was prepared for in such a situation, a lot of women, he knew, cried afterwards at what they considered their weakness in giving in, but this was no mere womanly sentiment, this was –

'What is it?' His own voice disturbed him, thin and dry, someone else's.

He heard her say, 'Some day I'll wake up and *I'll* be the princess.'

Her head had dropped on to her breast, her eyes lowered to her twisting fingers in her lap. Preparing to listen, he folded his bare legs in as sightly a position as he could manage, propping his head in his hands.

'I took to drink once. Brandy every night. I couldn't sleep without it.'

The possibility that it wasn't going to be as bad as he'd expected after all relaxed him, removed a layer or two of guilt.

She continued in the same low voice and now she was telling him about a man – there always was one, wasn't there? Someone called René, a West Indian doctor older than herself. She had been living with him, she wanted to leave him but couldn't break away, he always drew her back to him like 'a dog on a chain'.

A picture of the man, lean, cruel and very black, grew in his head as he listened to the catalogue of rows, the hysterical telephone calls and letters, a beating once, a threat of suicide. He found himself growing colder as she went on. How could she have fooled him, how had she been able to disguise all this despair behind the smiles, the gaiety, the innocence? He wanted her to stop now; a shutter should have descended moments ago enclosing everything pleasant for him to remember later. But he could see that she was going to pour all she had out and into him. He felt faint drowning sensations already.

Then the first unsettling shift began to appear in her recital. Images, physical, tugged at him for the first time, for even his idea of the other man up to now had been an unrealised one. Now he saw two labouring bodies in the sharpest detail. The thought that she had probably been comparing his performance with that of her black lover minutes earlier ate into him.

26

Her voice continued. She had become pregnant – *oh, God* – she had pleaded with the man, he had avoided her, she pursued him to his flat, his place of work. They'd had a showdown, he told her that it was her mess, she should clear it up and leave him alone. She described her desperation and loneliness and the London of bedsitters where solitary people sit with head in hand rose before him.

Then there began the worst part, slow in the telling, a descent into horror. And again he was made to realise that he might as well not be there, no allowance being made for his presence; her account of what took place in that one day and one night behind the locked door of her tiny flat was so much her own, not really meant to be shared. But in spite of this he was in there with her, in that flat, or rather, as time moved them on, in an inner, smaller room among the steam and the sound of ceaselessly running taps. He smelt and felt that bathroom, the bottle of gin, the tablets, the stained towels on the wet floor, the words in his ear leading his gaze cruelly on and on and over at last to the pale porcelain oval and what lay within – horrible, unspeakable, final. 'Oh, I want my baby, I want my baby,' she cried, and it was over.

A little while later he began to gather up the things with infinite precision. Each piece of rind, scrap of paper was stowed out of sight. He inspected the bruised rectangle of grass, when the rug was taken up, minutely, as though determined that as little trace of their presence as possible should remain after they had gone.

They drove back to the city in silence, rushing past the sluggish lines of out-of-town commuters sweltering in their cars. He dropped her off at the hostel, muttering a few clipped sentences. It was not goodbye, he would drive her to the airport the following day. Then he drove home.

Some distance away from his own house he stopped the car. He went over the interior, upholstery, floor, dashboard, pockets – even the roof surface – as carefully as he had examined the picnic place, and it seemed to him through his numbness that it wasn't quite the routine precaution he observed for his wife's benefit – it was something more, much more.

*

27

The following morning, true to his word, he took her to the plane and stood attentively by as she checked in tickets and baggage, then bore a cup of coffee over to her in the departure lounge and chatted beside her on the low leather seat. He even noted down her London address, saying that occasionally he had an excuse to travel over there, said he'd look her up. His performance, he decided, was a good one, marred only slightly by a tendency to look away a little too quickly but then she would probably put that down to the distractions of the crowded and noisy room, or even a deeper, more emotional reason.

At last her flight was called and he stood up. Taking her arm he moved her gently towards the queue shuffling down the covered ramp. Then the thing he dreaded most began to happen. She hesitated and turned to face him in the middle of all those people. His grip tightened, some deranged idea of force entering his mind, but then she said, 'Please. Don't worry. It's all right. *I'm* all right.' She smiled. 'I just want you to have this. I take it everywhere. As a souvenir – from me.'

She had dipped into her straw bag and now held out something loosely wrapped in paper. 'You don't have to open it now,' then, 'Goodbye', and she was merging into the cluster of travellers being sucked down the descent to the waiting plane. He watched her glossy legs until they disappeared from view.

He didn't think to look at what she had given him until he had got back to the city. Sitting there in the parked car he put his hand into his pocket and drew it out. The thing depressed easily to his touch, another toy of some sort. He took off the paper and looked at it. It was one of those rubbery little creatures known as Trolls. He knew the name because his class delighted in them, much to his mystification for their lifelike similarity to a shrunken human form had always disturbed him. The eyes were large and unnaturally bright, the hair black and wild, the tiny hands simian. He put it on the padded ledge in front of him and leaned on the wheel for a moment, his head in his hands.

For some reason he was feeling sick. He couldn't trace the cause, just felt the turning in his stomach. Then he looked at *it*, close to his face, and in one thump of realisation knew the full horror of what it reminded him of. Stumbling out of the car, he held the tiny smooth torso away from him. It felt moist and breathing because of the sweat on his hands. When he found a rubbish basket on a lamp standard he pushed the thing down deep, almost to the bottom, beneath the papers there. Then he returned to the car wiping each of his fingers carefully with a handkerchief. But it was some considerable time before he could bring himself to move off in the direction of home where his blonde wife was waiting for him.

The Temperate House

At Stamford Brook the train doors stayed apart and bird-song entered the compartment. Webster thought of the solitary warbler revelling in the dripping gardens beyond and that old air came into his head, the Delia Murphy version everyone back home seemed to have around the place, 'If I Were A Blackbird'. A memory of an ancient, high, cracked voice lingered and for a moment he felt pierced by an emotion he couldn't place. Then a girl with cockatoo crest and chalk white cheeks walked past the open door and the voice in his head died.

Slumped and sleeping in the opposite seat of the empty carriage was the one they called Denis in the pub, Denis the actor, who had once appeared in a television commercial for dog food – or was it tinned salmon? Webster hadn't seen it himself but somehow could visualise him standing there in his blazer and pale cords holding up the product. That had been some time ago, of course, and the gentlemanly attire had taken some hard wear since then, as had its owner.

At closing-time that afternoon the two of them had found themselves abandoned outside on the pavement and, despite the fact they had barely exchanged a nod in all the time they had been regulars, a bond of sorts had been formed there on this damp Sunday in summer. Brains numbed by Greene King, they both did their little stumbling dance; a red bus roared cruelly past inches away and terror united them. West London seemed foreign and hostile.

First to recover, the older man mumbled something about knowing a place and started off down Church Street but, at the drinking club near its foot, they pretended not to know him. Webster hung at the top of the stairs; he

30

invariably anticipated the worst, it was his nature and, when the actor came back up with an angry, mottled face, he manged to commiserate without actually saying anything. It was something he seemed to have perfected. By then, of course, he had resigned himself to the slow return by bus to his room; time for a sleep, a wash, then back once more to the place they had just come from. Pub life could be unrelenting; you couldn't afford to disappear from your particular haunt for even a short time, he had discovered that.

But Denis, as they called him, didn't seem to have done with him just yet. Sniffing the air he held up a hand in almost military fashion and, pointing in the direction of Barker's, set off again at the same rapid, unsteady pace. Webster felt he was expected to follow and he did so like a man with no will of his own. At the bottom of the hill both risked life and limb crossing against the lights, then on past the once great department store. Without a backward glance Denis swerved in under the Underground sign and Webster slackened pace. Well, he told himself, it seems the old fool was only heading for his train after all. But curiosity made him idle on until he was at the mouth of the arcade beside the paper-seller's pitch. He poked his head around and there he was in the middle of the concourse, waiting. Webster debated whether he should quietly melt into the crowds, but the image of that red face and those fierce blue eyes troubled him. Some sort of retribution seemed a possibility, though he didn't know why. He heard a shouted 'Hallo!' unmistakeable even at that distance, and his fate was sealed. Five minutes later he was heading south on a District line train beginning to feel angry with himself and the man opposite, who had fallen asleep the moment they had moved off.

Webster now stared out at the station where they lay becalmed. It could have been the country and, certainly, the green line that charted their route above the door did seem to be plunging dangerously to a point off the map where life, as he knew it, stopped. As far as he could recall he had never before travelled in the light on the Underground. That's why they called it that, after all. Deciding to cut his losses he stood up but the instant he did so the sleeper opposite opened a burning eye.

'Where are we?'

'Stamford Brook,' replied Webster, civilly enough.

'Stamford Brook!' barked the other as if in accusation and, sure enough, his next words were, 'Why did you let me drop off?'

Webster could think of nothing to say – he was so astonished – and by then the doors had closed and the train was picking up speed. He sat down and looked across at the other man who had now straightened himself up.

'I don't think I caught your name,' he asked.

'Tom.'

The blue eyes flashed a second time. 'Your *second* name.'

Webster hesitated fractionally then, 'Webster,' he murmured.

'My God! Mine's more Irish than yours! Brady! What d'you think of that, eh?'

Webster showed his teeth in what was meant to be a smile. At home no one had ever remarked on his name but over here he had found himself among a nation of dogs continually sniffing out everyone else's pedigree.

Nothing further was spoken until the train stopped at Kew, when Denis the actor stood up, swaying just a little, and Webster followed him out on to the neglected little platform. There was the scent of honeysuckle in the air. The rain had ceased. Surrendering their tickets, they went down the stairs and up and out into what looked like a village street. Past the rows of shops, all shut, except for an Asian newsagent's, and then the big houses began. Webster could recognise affluence when he saw it and he wondered which of these fine detached dwellings was to be their destination. Could the man at his side be one of those who, for some reason, pretended poverty? No one in this country was ever what they seemed. For a moment he felt a foolish pride in

32

having been singled out from all the other regulars in the
Grapes for a rare glimpse into an Englishman's home. But
then that small, inner voice he knew so well murmured to
him of caution.

As they passed one of the villas the sound of piano
practice drifted out to them and Webster had a clear picture
of a high-ceilinged room and a child, a girl, pigtailed and
serious, bent over a keyboard. All the things he'd ever read
about this place had a habit of turning out to be exactly as
he'd imagined.

Denis strode on without change of pace until the end of
the avenue. Then he proceeded to cross the main road and
Webster began to feel something must be wrong; he was
heading for the black and gold gates of the Gardens.
Straight to the turnstiles he marched and handed the
attendant some money. The turnstile clicked, passing him
through while Webster stood where he was. A sudden image
of a grinning chorus in the pub had assailed him. He felt
certain now that all of them knew things about this man that
he didn't.

'*Come on!*'

A ticket was being waved in the air. For some reason it
seemed to draw Webster almost hypnotically, that pale
scrap, for his feet carried him across the road and down the
short approach to the turnstiles. The attendant pressed
some hidden mechanism and the metal bars gave way under
the barest pressure of his body. Denis stood a few yards
away still holding the ticket aloft.

'Good!' he bawled. 'Good! Glad you made it!' and the
attendant turned away with a grin.

Webster felt the drink renew a hold on him. He was
young, strong and proud of his capacity yet suddenly he
yearned after that afternoon sleep in the single room in
Willesden. Like an animal he needed to withdraw to his lair.
He thought of all the possibilities close at hand. Often on his
way home on afternoons such as this he would pass through
another park, nothing like this, of course, just one of those
secret little patches of London green, and he would see his

33

countrymen sprawling there with their *Independents* and a transistor shared between four or five of them. If he closed his eyes the footballing commentary on the radios would transport him back in time and distance to a country crossroads. But he always walked quickly on without a sideways glance for there lay the easy decline, the sentiment of the backward look.

Denis said, 'I want to show you something,' taking his arm. 'Something you should see for yourself.' The sun had come out, thirstily sucking up the wet from every flat surface.

The voice had lost much of its militancy and, looking down at his sleeve, Webster saw an old man's hand suddenly, speckled brown as a gull's egg. Together they moved down the path between the steaming banks of vegetation like father and son. The phrase had entered Webster's consciousness without warning then melted away like the moisture on the leaves.

Their route took them past massed rhododendrons with Latin names, their smell reminding Webster of demesnes back home, then a giant flagstaff to the right (*225 feet, Douglas fir, presented by the Government of British Columbia*, he read).

Further on, through the dotted trees, he caught a glimpse of something foreign and fantastic, a Chinese pagoda, many-tiered and rising from the clipped English sward. Could this be what he had been brought all this way to see? The man at his side could quite easily have lived in the East, he had a colonial look about him; was this, then, nothing more than a sentimental pilgrimage he felt like sharing with someone else for once, someone from the pub? But no, for again Webster felt himself being steered on along the path until they rounded a bend and there, rising from its gentle elevation in the heart of that extravagant yet ordered landscape, was the great glasshouse. The man at his side stopped, and Webster did so too. He knew he was expected to marvel but again, like all those other famous sights, it was somehow as he'd always imagined it to be.

34

Denis said, 'The first and foremost of its kind. I just thought you really ought to see it, that's all.'

There was a catch in his voice and Webster knew suddenly that he was going to have to see this thing, whatever it was, through to the end. They stood there gazing in silence at the ornate structure glittering in the sun like a vast, elongated birthday cake iced with glass.

'Designed by a countryman of yours. Did you know that? Burton. Decimus Burton. Name like yours, as well.'

Webster visualised someone distinguished in black poring over blueprints in the open air, an army of workmen waiting anxiously for his word of command. They were his countrymen too, as Denis so quaintly put it, but nobody had told them that. The man at the trestle table murmured something to an assistant at his side who relayed it to another lower in rank and on the word travelled until, finally, it reached the men leaning on their spades. They gave a great cry and rushed forward to cut the first sod.

'Of course the Palm House is the one they all come to see,' and Denis pointed far to the right over the trees. 'But I've always preferred this.'

Webster waited for some further confidence but the man with the soldierly bearing stood staring ahead of him as though he could see through all that distant glass to something only he could perceive. One or two people were moving about in front of the structure and, even at this remove, they had an indecisive look about them. There was an open doorway that seemed to draw them. As they watched, two women in hats hovered, then disappeared inside.

'Come,' said Denis. 'It's a world all its own. You'll see, you'll see,' and they set off.

There had been a big decaying house behind gates and its own walls near where Webster used to live. Much of it had been burned down for political reasons before he was born but there still remained the shell of a conservatory, a large one by country standards. Perched on top of the old walls he could just make out its damaged glazing, but vines and a peach tree were reputed still to grow there because of the southerly aspect. He had often wondered what it must be like to stand in that artificial climate.

A flight of stone steps led him up, then through this arched doorway and suddenly he had entered that imagined world of his childhood. Moist heat enveloped him, there were strong, unsettling scents and, most unexpected of all, the sound of birds. The glass seemed to magnify and coarsen their cries and he looked up half-hoping for a gaudy flash of plumage.

Chile, Argentina, he read; they had turned left and were in the South American section. Water trickled constantly and, from its island, rose a great palm tree, almost to the roof.

The two women he had seen entering the place earlier stood gazing aloft as though hoping for a glimpse of coconuts. They were West Indian and wore Sunday hats and white gloves. One still carried her hymnbook.

Denis said in a loud voice, 'Chilean Wine Palm. Largest greenhouse plant in the entire world,' and they turned to stare at him. 'Can I be of assistance?' he asked.

The tall one with the gold-rimmed glasses giggled; the other, short and squat, spoke with a voice like a man's.

'Barbados. We'se lookin' for Barbados.'

Denis bowed. 'I think you'll find the Caribbean section further along to your right. If not, try the tropical Palm House.'

The one who had spoken glared at him, a natural sceptic if ever Webster saw one, and it was left to her friend to say, 'You'se most kind,' before moving off.

Denis dropped down on to a low retaining wall and mopped his brow with a red and white spotted handkerchief as if the effect of his gallantry had exhausted him.

Webster meanwhile was standing looking up at the narrow gangway that ran all the way round under the roof. He could see a spiral staircase giving access at the far end. It drew him the way it would a child. Denis must have sensed something of this, for he said suddenly, 'Where are you

36

going?' even though he hadn't yet made a move.

'Up there,' he said.

'But, there are so many –'

'I just want to see what it's like from up there.' Webster heard his voice take on an authoritative note, much to his surprise.

He began to walk off along the narrow path under the hanging greenery until he reached the foot of the white-painted iron staircase. He started to climb, and a feeling of elation rose in him with each tread. He felt the heat mount, as well, the closer he got to the glass. At the top he took several deep breaths even though he was young and fit and wasn't winded in the least. It was just his way of expressing the pleasure that suddenly filled every part of him. With legs apart, he leaned on the iron rail and looked down on the rain-forest spread out for him below, noting with pleasure every subtle gradation of colour and foliage. For the first time he saw fat, red and gold fish in the pool. Almost directly beneath was the crown of a thick palm, its fronds strongly spreading, feathery, yet so dense that he felt if he jumped they would quite easily bear him up. Webster laughed out loud at the strange thoughts crowding his head. Then there came a voice to invade this private paradise.

'Webster! I say, Webster!'

Webster gritted his teeth. Looking down he saw old Denis at the foot of the staircase and he knew he had no choice but to wait until the other made his slow ascent. Deliberately he kept his gaze averted, but it was impossible to avoid the sound of that laboured climb. He recognised a certain amount of genuine distress but felt there was an element of counterfeit there as well, to capture sympathy and attention. Damn the old fraud, he thought.

Out of the corner of his eye he caught a glimpse of a hand, then a grey head, as both rose slowly above the fretted metalwork.

'I'd love a drink. Wouldn't you?'

Webster held his peace as the other hung panting on the rail by his side.

37

'I had a feeling you'd appreciate this experience. You seemed different from the others – correct me if I'm wrong – Declan, and that rowdy lot...'

Webster allowed his gaze to travel over the soothing arrangement of tropical greens below. He wanted to shut out the voice at his elbow for he had the terrible suspicion that if he paid attention he would learn something he didn't wish to hear.

'Happiest year of my life spent in your country. With a touring company. Quite a well-known one, too. No rubbish, and full houses every night. Not a whisper; you could do *anything* with those people. Retained that sense of wonder, you see. Not like here. Never play in Middlesborough...' He gave a harsh laugh that ended in a sort of choking gasp.

Webster concentrated hard on the harmonies of nature beneath his feet.

'In one place, I remember, we were doing the Scottish play and afterwards this young chap came backstage. Said it had changed his life. Tears in his eyes, that sort of thing. Had to be an actor, just *had* to be. Of course I tried to dissuade him, but I could see it was no use. Poor boy followed us round every hall in the country. Always wondered whatever became of him. About your age. Nice, well set-up country lad; certainly all right in the looks department...'

Webster wondered what the Scottish play was, but the question only involved part of his mind. Deeper, stronger, was his own memory of such a troupe that had once come to his own village. Magic there had been none; all he recalled was tattered scenery, holed costumes and pathetic acting, and the company wearing full make-up in the street, the men as well as the women. The star of the company, about Denis's age – all wig and dyed hair – so the story went, would offer money after the show to anyone who would let him take their thing in his mouth. Webster saw the old man's claw close to his young, healthy hand on the rail. How long, he wondered, before that came within brushing distance of his own flies.

38

He was wearing a woollen pullover next to his skin and, quite suddenly, he pulled it over his head and knotted it about his waist. He knew it gave him the look of a navvy, even though no one was to know he really worked in a biscuit factory on the North Circular. The sultry air bathed his body and Denis quickly gasped then coughed with deep embarrassment, but that was only music to Webster's ears. Grasping the rail until his muscles bulged, for a moment he was a bare-breasted mariner on the bridge of his own craft. Then he walked quickly off without a backward look, the perforated iron springing under his stride.

At the far end of the gangway he halted to take up his skipper's stance once more. Old Denis had the spotted hanky out by now and was anxiously scanning the paths below in case someone might chance to look up and see the pair of them. But Webster was thinking of those men with the spades again, that forgotten army who had sweated to raise this glass temple to an alien respectability and had then dispersed without trace, back to those single rooms all over the city. For this tiny moment he was their representative, even though he had an English surname and his job, in truth, only involved sweeping broken rusks from a factory floor in Neasden.

Lifting his head, he looked about him at the glass, so much of it within touching distance. Already he was seeing his name in the local paper on the page devoted to drinking offences. The fact, of course, was he'd never felt more sober in his life, but why complicate things.

As he was about to raise his clenched fist he heard a cry and, turning, saw Denis half-way along the gangway, the spotted handkerchief moving like a flag of distress in his hand. His face held an expression of panic. He seemed to sway before dropping to his knees. Webster stood looking at him. Down below a couple had appeared, a man and his wife in tourist garb, and stopped to stare. They deflected Webster's wrath – the man wore a particularly senseless baseball cap in orange – and, because of this, he found himself heading towards the pathetic heap on the gangway instead of away as he'd intended, for he had spotted another way down by another identical spiral staircase.

Old Denis looked up out of bleary eyes as he approached. He seemed to have aged considerably. 'Can't seem to get up. Vertigo. Silly of me, I know.'

Webster wanted to laugh despite the other's condition. It was just that the words and their delivery could have come straight from any bad old black and white film, the sort they usually showed at exactly this time of the afternoon on television.

Reaching down, he got a grip under both armpits and lifted him to his knees. Together they began struggling towards the head of the staircase. Webster tried hard not to think of those elderly paws clutching his bare back.

Half-way down the stairs – it seemed to him they weren't going to make the bottom – he propped his burden on one of the steps and took several deep breaths – he needed them this time – while Denis looked up at him.

'My legs,' he murmured. 'They appear to have lost all feeling. Most odd.'

A terrible suspicion entered Webster's mind. For the second time that day he seemed to see all those faces in the pub barely able to contain their mirth. Then he thought of how he had stripped himself to the waist so eagerly and went cold at the thought.

'Come on,' he said roughly. 'We can't sit about here all day. We've been in this place far too long as it is.'

Denis made a desperate effort to stand and Webster was able somehow to manhandle him down and around the remaining twists in the stairs until they reached the ground. He steered him along the path towards the open air and, as they passed the American couple, some cruelty in him made him call out, 'Never see a drunk man before?' He felt old Denis stiffen in his grasp.

There was a bench outside and they both sat there waiting for everything that had happened to recede. The sun had slid to a point where it turned the glass at their back to sheet gold but neither of them was in the mood to register the

40

phenomenon. Webster looked straight ahead at the distant trees while Denis studied the creases in his trousers.

'Ridiculous business, I do apologise. I hope you don't let it spoil it for you, seriously, I do; this place, I mean. It's part of a great tradition, you see. Yours, as well. Belongs to all of us, and I did so want to show it to you. Not just the plants, wonderful as they are, brought back from every corner of the globe, and sometimes at great risk, too, but the whole idea, the sheer breadth of vision. I mean, can't you see it, those men and their genius...'

But Webster was still gazing at the trees. He was looking for ghosts, his own army of ghosts in muddy moleskins, silent and watching and redundant. For a moment he thought he caught a glimpse of something out there but then, as the man at his side continued to talk, they receded. Eventually, Webster said, 'The pubs will be open soon. Come on, Denis,' and so they rose together and set out for the gates. Perhaps those other men, they had never existed, after all, except in his imagination.

Monkey Nuts

It was almost a month after her mother died when she finally got round to looking into the old tin trunk and there, under the layers of ancient *Gazettes* lining the bottom, came upon that paper triangle with its red and blue airmail edging. Taking it out to the light she read, 119 North And Maple, Towanda, PA 18848. There was no sender's name. Just the address staring up at her in a faded black hand. The house was quiet except for the rapid movement of the clock and, as she sat there holding her discovery, it seemed to tick even faster as if competing with the beat of blood in her head. Then she became cold as ice. Rising, she went to the oak bureau where she kept her savings book, took it out and sat staring at the inked numerals, even though she knew that final amount to the penny. On the opened page she laid the faded triangle. Something magical about the combination of those two sets of handwriting, one feminine, exact – it could have been her own – the other, an old man's scrawl, impressed her deeply. Together they added up to something so momentous in her life that, for a second time, her temples pounded and she wondered if she was going to end up a victim of the same circulatory ailment that had carried her mother off. But the mirror above the bureau reflected her face and, of course, it looked just the same as always, sallow, tending to oiliness, not a bit like her mother's much admired roses and cream complexion. It stood to reason which side of the family she took after, for all the Beattys were redheads and now, for the first time in her life, she had the means of proving the point.

Three weeks later, still amazed at herself, she was on a wide-bodied jet trying to read the instructions for the use of headsets. The stethoscope, as they called it, lay in her lap but she couldn't bring herself to push those soft rubber tips into her ears. All around her other people with no such qualms, it seemed, were gently smiling with closed eyes, listening to 'Man of La Mancha', Channel 7 or 'The Planets' on Classical Selection or even 'Wichita Linesman' on Channel 1. Oblivious at thirty thousand feet, some were even plugged into the soundtracks of the three films running silently and simultaneously up at the front of the plane. It wasn't meanness that stopped her from paying to see George C. Scott in *Patton* – she had drawn out most of the money in her account for this trip, after all – it was just the idea of those things in her ears cutting off her consciousness.

The question of hygiene didn't really arise, although there was a man three rows behind, asleep, snoring and, to all appearances, dead drunk, and the thought of those ears and the likelihood of sharing, even at its remotest, made her feel queasy. She stole another glance at him. His mouth hung open and he had spilled food down his shirt and tie. What made her take such notice of him was the fact that she was almost positive he was from her home town. If it wasn't the one everyone called Monkey Nuts then he must have a double, and the idea of a replica of that shambling creature perhaps speaking French or Italian, or even having an American twang made her smile despite herself.

From her position at the back of the shop, she would see him propped up outside Simpson's, the newsagent's opposite, one leg bent back so that his boot sole seemed bonded to the wall. He could sustain such a position for hours on end. And then, before leaving to go home, he would always walk across to peer in at them through the glass. From her eyrie above the customers' heads, she would catch a glimpse of his face between the dummies, jaws steadily grinding away. She knew what it was that brought him over; the old-fashioned canisters that sped, carrying cash from the counters up to where she sat perched and then back again with the change. Old Mr Ferris had refused to part with them. Every so often the man at the window

43

would stop chewing and she could almost see the struggle going on within him. It was cruel of her, she knew, but at such times she would deliberately linger over the ritual of charging the burnished cylinder with its freight of coins wrapped in its own pink receipt. She would also delay that final pull on the polished wooden handle until the man outside in the street looked as though he would be able to contain himself no longer and must burst into the shop. But she knew he would never do such a thing, no matter how long she kept the canister swaying in its cage above her head. Finally, of course, she would release it, almost casually, and it would wing down the wire and the chewing would resume.

No, she told herself, how could it be the one the children followed about the town, how could it be? What would someone like that be doing on a jumbo on its way to Kennedy Airport?

One of the stewardesses, blonde and smiling, as they all seemed to be, came down the aisle and, stopping at the sleeping figure, unfolded a baby-blue blanket and tucked it around him. With a quick and delicate touch, she had transformed a sleeping man into a red-faced infant. Some of the passengers obviously enjoyed these little attentions. She'd overheard one old American in a plaid jacket say to his wife, 'It really is just like flying in an elephant, honey,' and she saw what he meant, the rightness of such a name for an aeroplane, that comforting and most reliable of nursery animals. People needed to feel like that, more than anything, she reckoned, suspended all those thousands of feet up in the air.

Then the time came when all three screens at the front went back to being grey and silent again and the voice over the loudspeaker told them they were making their final descent. All about her people were becoming animated and friendly, peering out of the windows at the unseen city far below, and for the first time since she had found that torn-off flap of paper and its shaky message, she became frightened of what she had done but, more importantly, of

44

what lay ahead. All these other people already unbuckling seat belts, despite the red warning signs, had destinations in mind, they had families and friends waiting to meet them when they touched down. Although she had never flown before she had a sudden premonition of herself lost and alone in the midst of a dense crowd of travellers extravagantly hugging and kissing one another.

She took the piece of paper out of her handbag and stared at it in an attempt to dispel the image. But it only made things worse. Not even a name, just a place, foreign-sounding, and what was 18848? Could she have saved herself all this terror, not to mention expense, by merely lifting up a phone? But no, it had to be done this way; a strange voice crackling on a line that stretched three thousand miles would never have satisfied her. The ache had been with her all her life in some form or other, and when she found the address at the bottom of her mother's old trunk it had started up again, the tears and that feeling of having lost something she'd never ever had.

Standing in the aisle with the other passengers she saw that the man with the airline blanket about him was still sound asleep. The queue began to move and her heart beat quickened as she shuffled nearer, but his face was turned to the window; all she could see was a red nape that seemed to bear the recent marks of a barber's carelessness. As the travellers ahead of her filed past she noticed them grinning and she suddenly felt ashamed for him and herself and their poor town. These people with their cameras and smart travel bags would see it as a joke if ever they went there, in much the same way as they reacted to the man still wrapped and sleeping like an infant. But then she told herself, no, you must stop this line of thought, Myrna, you know fine well this is a rank stranger with nothing whatever to do with you or your home or country, for that matter.

The lecture seemed to do her good for she straightened herself up and, when the time came to go past him, she did so without a second or even a first glance. However, just as she was drawing away, she felt something small and round

45

and brittle crunch under her foot, but she didn't look down or back to see what it was. She wouldn't allow herself to do so.

In the terminal building the young man with the moustache at the Immigration counter looked at her steadily then down at her passport photograph; up, down, up, until she felt clammy under her clothes.

'Is the purpose of your visit business or pleasure, Miss Beatty?'

'Pleasure,' she stammered, but the word sounded fraudulent somehow.

He looked at her sternly for a moment then finally handed over her passport.

'Have a nice trip,' he smiled, showing dazzling white teeth before turning to the next passenger, and she felt as though a searchlight had been suddenly switched away from her. How could someone in a job like his – it was really rather ordinary – look like a film star? As they all did, all the young men at their counters, even the policemen in their beautifully ironed blue short-sleeved shirts. And who sewed their badges on so straight? Forty years earlier her own mother must have felt something of the same wonder, but it was only much later that Myrna was to recognise the coincidence.

Now she was standing on American soil, free of all formalities at last, and the scene she had imagined so vividly on the aeroplane was taking place all about her. Her new leather suitcase rested on the marble floor on its four hard little bumps and she took up her stance beside it as though she might have to relinquish it at any moment to one of these yelling, laughing, weeping people. She realised now why the young men with their moustaches had seemed so stern and unforgiving. Their job was to stem this tide and all about her was the living proof that the task was an impossible one.

She saw a family of dark Latin-looking people kissing and shouting in a huddle, an old man in white robes being led by the hand through the crowds by a small boy, a woman collapsed and panting on a bench while her family fanned her with pieces of cardboard they had wrenched from their luggage. The terrible heat she was experiencing must come from all these people, she decided. It was like no other heat she had ever felt before, frightening and foreign, and must surely have travelled here with them.

Although it was a rash act, she realised that, she headed for the exit doors. Once outside there might be no hope of ever getting back in again, but she had to breathe fresh air and convince herself that there really was firm ground out there and a sky above, just as there was back home. At her approach the grey-tinted sheets of glass sucked angrily apart and it was as if a great mouth had opened and breathed on her. Without thinking she stepped forward, the glass at her back resealed itself, and sweat seemed to burst from every pore of her body.

Although it was noon the sky was black, water roared in the gutters from a recent thunderstorm and the policemen who strode about, all over six foot tall, black, and blowing whistles, wore wet ankle-length oilskins. The oilskins were black too and the sight of these dark figures with their angry faces left her without hope of any kind. She saw herself standing on this one spot paralysed and speechless until the final collapse took place. A line of battered yellow taxis crawled ever closer and she knew she must take one despite the cost, it was her only hope. Other passengers were climbing into them, even poor people, but it was hard for her to feel any advantage. The fact that she could speak English and they couldn't in some perverse way made her more vulnerable. She had seen these taxi-drivers on television and knew them for what they were. Admittedly they were played by actors, but all their sarcasm and aggression had to be based on some sort of reality.

Then one of the yellow cabs was right beside her and the back door swung open. She stood staring until one of the policemen rushed up and blew his whistle at her as though his anger made it impossible for him to even speak, and as she got into the taxi, it suddenly came to her that these

47

giants in their black oilskins weren't policemen at all but porters, an infinitely inferior job, and so they rushed around in a permanent fury.

'Where to, lady?'

The back seat had a shiny transparent cover and already she felt fastened to it like an insect on flypaper – the colour was the same as well, a faded old gold. She tried to move closer to the stiff, uncaring neck, but couldn't.

'Okay, take as long as you like, lady. *I* ain't goin' nowhere.' So they were like that after all, she thought.

'I want to catch a bus to Towanda. A Greyhound bus.' Her voice came out as a squeak and she didn't know if he could hear or not. From the back of his head he looked younger than she expected. Was that an earring?

'Towanda? Greyhound?'

'Yes,' she said in a much louder voice. 'Towanda, Pennsylvania.'

'Ah,' he said, 'we're gettin' closer by the minute.'

She saw him glance at the racing meter as though he judged it necessary to reinforce this heavy sarcasm. For the very first time she felt a quickening of her old spirit. After all she had money in her purse and a responsible position in life. Everyone in the shop knew she was indispensable, even old Mr Ferris, despite his silly pretence.

'I suppose you've never really been outside New York.'

The driver didn't reply, but the cab began to pick up speed. They were passing a huge sign with a smiling old white-haired Southern gentleman on it. He was holding up a chicken leg. It was the first familiar thing she had encountered since she had got on that plane.

'I've been in every capital and country of Europe, lady, including your own,' and he began to sing a passable rendition of 'The Londonderry Air'. When he finished she knew she should say something for she had the feeling he had a well polished repertoire of national songs to surprise every one of his passengers.

'Your voice must be trained,' she said.

'You know what my dream is? Go on, guess. Have a guess.'

48

She began to slide her fingers under her thighs to break the bond holding her to the shiny plastic of the seat. Could he see *everything* of her in his tilted mirror? Occasionally she caught glimpses of one of his eyes and a strip of forehead beneath the leather cap.

He said, 'La Scala. They have the best teachers in the world there. You think I'm gonna drive a cab all my life? Get old behind a wheel? Fat chance, lady, fat chance,' and he laughed bitterly.

There was nothing she felt she could say. She looked out of the window at the dereliction they were speeding past, so many rusting cars piled on top of one another, sometimes as many as six deep. Back home there was a dump at the edge of town, but nothing like this; it was like a toy in comparison and children did indeed play there in perfect safety.

After a time the driver said, 'You got relatives or somethin' in Pennsylvania?' and it was as though he had been observing her all along and had seen right through her.

She murmured something and then he said, 'I got no one in the whole wide world. Never had and never felt the need to, neither, if you must know.' He began to talk about his start in life in an orphanage, then the navy, then driving a cab here in New York. He wasn't bitter, but he reckoned if he'd had real parents like other kids he would probably have been very big in the operatic world by now, very big. She marvelled at how a complete stranger could tell another stranger his entire life-story so easily and without any sense of shame. Where she came from you only found such things out by stealth and sly and patient observation over the years.

'Oh, yes,' he said with a sigh, 'it's dog eat dog out there, lady. Dog eat dog.'

It was a phrase she'd heard hundreds of times before but, because of his accent, it seemed to reveal its true meaning for the first time. For one dangerous moment she thought of confiding in this man, of telling him they had something in common, but then her old suspicious nature reasserted itself. She let him talk away knowing full well, of course, that it was only a ploy to distract her from the sight of that

49

flickering dial on his right side which was running away with her hard-earned savings. But she didn't care, she didn't care, and even when they reached the bus station – she was to take a Trailways, not a Greyhound – and he stopped the meter at what seemed a colossal figure she climbed out of the back of the cab and handed him the fare and a fine tip without another thought.

The summer's gone and all the roses falling,
It's you, it's you must go and I must bide.

He serenaded her briefly through the open window before driving off and it was only then she noticed he had a harelip and was older than she was.

The bus had windows permanently tinted against the glare so that the landscape it slid through had a grey and alien look. There were trees and fields and painted wooden farmhouses but she didn't recognise anything familiar about them. Even the animals looked like something from a colouring book that had strayed into the hands of a depressed child. There was a toilet aboard the bus but she held out against using it: the deep seats and dim lights, that burned even though it was afternoon, induced apathy and a feeling of numbness. Many of the other passengers were asleep. They lay across the seats or up against the windows without thought of how they must appear and although her mind was tired she wondered if she could ever become like that if she lived long enough with all this heat, not caring, just letting it have its way. She'd always imagined that people from other countries with such seasons had evolved their own defences but the sleepers looked as though they were as unprepared as she was. They all looked poorer than she was as well, she could tell that, despite the fact that they were American.

She remembered a silly saying, 'The land of the mighty dollar and the ten cent cigar'. It didn't mean anything, just something picked up from some film or other by one of the men and boys who would lie around the big beech tree in the summer evenings waiting for the racing pigeons to come home to roost. She would watch them from her bedroom window and listen to the sudden explosive laughter until only that and the lighted tips of their cigarettes remained as an indication of their presence. She dreamed of America, just as they did, only hers were secret dreams, forbidden, too, because once her mother had heard her talking in her sleep and had shaken her awake and made her purge her dream with a cold wet flannel. But she continued to dream secretly and silently, one dream in particular, always that same one.

Closing her eyes now on the travelling interior, the remembered tableau swam obediently into focus, the man, the dog, the little girl. The man threw a stick, the dog chased it, her younger self clapped excitedly, perhaps too excitedly, because the tall man with the crew-cut in the checked shirt gathered her up and pointed after the racing terrier. Its name was Topsy and it was a real scamp. One morning she had come down early in bare feet and discovered it as a puppy in a basket under the Christmas tree. She had sat down on the carpet there and then and held it to her while it licked her face. It was a moment to remember all her life, the little girl in the dream told herself, she would always remember this one moment while the rest of the house slept on.

The bus drew to a halt with a hiss of its air brakes and the soft coloured scene dimmed like the dying of a flame. It was their first stop and an old couple helped one another down to stand shakily in a patch of dusty gravel outside some sort of roadside shop. An enamel sign caught her eye. 'Chew Red Man Tobacco', above a chipped and flaking life-size Indian looking straight at her. The eyes seemed to follow her as the bus moved off.

They stopped in several small towns after that; all had their population and altitude printed on a board on the outskirts. These modest numerals were a comfort. After all she came from a place not much larger in its complement of

51

souls, but then the hideous thought came to her that the place she was seeking might be very different, a hell-hole of furnaces and coal tips, because hadn't she read somewhere that this was a state that produced such things. A half-remembered litany from school geography echoed in her head and she distinctly saw men with blackened faces and lunch-tins under their arms surging out through great iron gates. They looked sullen and violent at the same time and all had names that were European and unpronounceable.

The scenery beyond the windows however continued to retain its rural quality and at last at four o'clock they passed a sign that said 'Towanda Welcomes You'. She wasn't quick enough to make out the population figure or the height above sea-level, either, but soon it became obvious that this was a small and manageable town like all the others they had passed through.

She got to her feet and made her way to the front of the bus. The doors parted and she stepped down with her new suitcase in her hand on to the land of her dreams, literally. Then the bus disappeared with a low and threatening roar and she was left standing in a silence so unsettling that she made an involuntary stumbling movement in the direction that big and dusty vehicle had taken. Panic seized her in its clammy grip.

She looked around for a sign of life but found none. She scanned the shop fronts but could see no movement behind any of the windows. There were parked cars but all were empty. Not even a dog nosed about. She looked at her watch. Had she adjusted it properly to accommodate the time change? It seemed more like noon than five past four. She thought senselessly of Gary Cooper and his long, suffering face in that famous film. Dust and heat and everyone staying indoors. But this wasn't the Wild West, she told herself. There were petrol pumps and a tarmacadamed road and those things on four legs that looked like rubbish bins but she now knew to be postboxes. There was a Woolworth's too, in the distance, and that familiar red and gold lettering allayed some of her dread. She began walking towards it for no other reason. Past a chemist's, a baby's-wear shop, a gun and fishing-tackle store, all dark inside, then a window with a dead neon sign that said 'Cocktails'. It was early closing, something so obvious, yet it had never struck her, her of all people. She thought of her own place of work with nostalgia, that glassed-in eyrie with its old revolving chair and her own electric kettle and supply of ginger-snaps, the cosiest of worlds where she was queen.

A rush of tears assailed her, the first, it so happened, since she had set foot in this awful country, and just then a voice said, 'Looks like a storm comin' up, if I'm not mistaken.'

She saw an old man with a friendly face sitting inside a doorway in the shade. Although she knew it had been no more than a passing politeness she pretended otherwise and dropped her suitcase with a sigh.

'Half-day?' she said and regretted it in the same moment.

'Some rain would sure be appreciated.'

She knew he hadn't understood the question but the time had come for her to assert herself, otherwise she'd go under for good.

'Do you happen to know of an hotel where I might find a room?' for she had left all that to fate, hoping that her innocence would protect her just like a baby in the back seat of a car when catastrophe strikes.

The old man said, 'This is only a small country place, ma'am. We ain't got nuthin' fancy like that hereabouts.'

He looked at her slyly to gauge her reaction but she kept her face stiff so as to give nothing away. She knew his type, knew that false modesty of old. Men like him sat day in, day out perfecting their wiles, waiting for some stranger to come along to outsmart.

As if reading her thoughts, he said, 'Leastways, we ain't got no Hilton or Sheraton, nuthin' grand of that sort.'

She picked up her suitcase, glancing around with impatience.

'But there *is* a Howard Johnson. I ain't never been there. No call at my age.'

If he thought that would soften her, the old goat was

gravely mistaken. She waited, clicking her tongue, and he said, 'Keep on a'goin' on this side of the street a good half-mile. It's just beyond Ira Hatfield's gas station.'

He called this last direction after her, but she was on her way, moving briskly despite the humidity and the beginnings of a headache. The first small victory was hers at last and she was determined to savour it to the full.

Forty minutes later she was congratulating herself a second time; she had just taken her first American shower in her own suite – to call it a room would be to belittle it needlessly. The bathroom she stood in was larger than her own living room at home, the carpet was thick and of a lustrous blue, it even extended itself up the side of the bath, the tiles and mirrors showed not a smear, but best and strangest of all was the water itself that gushed softly at a touch. Seemingly treated in some miraculous fashion, a million tiny bubbles mingled with its flow from the taps, it lathered with ease and, although she had never thought of water as having colour before, this had a pale almost translucent greyness.

She dried herself on one of the big fluffy bath towels and looked at herself in the full-length mirror. It was a rare experience. In her mother's house such a sight would have been regarded as indecent. All the people she knew only ever saw pieces of themselves. It was the way they were. Frankly she was surprised at what stared back at her, and more than a little pleased as well, if the truth were known. Breasts, waistline, thighs, calves – the whole inventory – was more than satisfactory for someone nudging forty, she told herself. She also told herself to stop the habit of acting like someone much older than she really was. That was another fault of the people back home.

Feeling quite skittish by now, she put on new underwear and the green Courtelle trouser-suit she had bought specially for the trip. She moved about the bedroom in her stockinged feet enjoying the feeling of possession for, already, even in this short space of time, everything about the place seemed familiar somehow. For instance, weren't those prints on the wall of girls in Bavarian peasant costume just the sort of thing she herself would have an eye for? She gave herself a last look of approval in the glass and felt a quickening of anticipation at what lay ahead.

At the desk downstairs she asked for North And Maple and, after an embarrassed delay, someone was found in the kitchen who knew where it was. A tired-looking girl with lank hair said that was in the South Township and 'would be real hard to find'. She stood there picking her spots and yawning in her white overall while the young manager fidgeted. He knew there was nothing he could do to make the girl more forthcoming and Myrna could see that as well. But she was feeling confident and relaxed after her ablutions and the memory of herself reflected so sympathetically in the peach-tinted mirror upstairs, so she strolled out into the early evening with a careless wave of her hand.

She walked out under the sign that said Howard Johnson Motor Lodge and, despite being on foot, felt no trace of inferiority. As she strolled towards the heart of the town it was clear that life had returned after the long day's sleep. Lights had come on and cars moved about. Occasionally one would come up behind her, slow down, then accelerate past and away with that squealing sound that seemed to be obligatory on this continent. The people in cars looked out at her but she walked on holding her new handbag clasped tightly to her side. She felt very aware of everything about her, the strange scents, the light deepening to a blue she'd never seen before, the insects that whirred in concert. It was like being in a film and she was at its centre, the mysterious star about to fulfil her destiny.

She walked past the 'Cocktails' sign which now glowed ruby red against a curtain of darker velvet. In a nearby supermarket women moved about pushing trolleys twice the size of the ones at home. She came upon two housewives chatting on the pavement beside one of these great wire-mesh chariots piled high with groceries. Both wore jeans, cut off and frayed above fat dimpled knees, and metal curlers were bunched in their hair. When she asked politely

55

for directions they stared at her, shifting their chewing gum from one side of their mouth to the other and slowly taking her in with their dull eyes.

'North And Maple, honey?' one of them said, and she replied, yes, that was correct.

They looked at one another. 'That's South Township, ain't it, Dolores?'

Her friend nodded. 'Sure is.'

They stood there arrested in thought until she spoke again, 'Is it far?'

The taller one said, 'Ain't that it's far. More out of the way. Ain't you got a car, honey?'

'No,' she said, made at last to feel the shame of such a lack. After a sigh the one who had called her 'honey' explained the route she must take; it didn't sound complicated in the least and, thanking them, she walked away feeling their eyes still on her. She thought of those huge globular behinds straining that well-washed denim and how they must surely be feeling envious of her own trim retreating figure. But deep inside her another voice, more cynical than that, told her that these people always felt pity for anyone who wasn't like themselves. She'd already seen enough of this country to realise the truth of that.

Veering away from the main street, as she had been instructed, Myrna came to a river bank and walked past decaying rows of warehouses with weeds sprouting from their roofs. She had reached that part of town the community had turned its back on. The thought cheered her, for there was a similar area back home full of broken windows and rusting machinery silent since the days of the linen boom. The road took her on past old wooden houses that must have been grand once, curlicued and ornate as wedding cakes. But now on their porches people sprawled in broken-down armchairs and settees which looked as though they were waiting to be collected for the dump. Many of the people who stared at her as she went past were negroes. They had a listless air that might have been because of the day's heat, but she had the feeling that it came from

56

something much more deep-seated than that. She began to wonder how far she would have to go before she came upon a sign, for the idea of having to ask assistance from any of these sullen observers was unthinkable. Even the dogs, stretched and panting in front of the houses, had an ill-natured look about them.

Then she reached a point where the road was at its worst. Ahead lay a jungle of head-high yellow reeds; to the left was the river. She took a narrow path to the right, all that was left to her and, nailed to the trunk of a tree, she saw what looked like an old tea tray someone had been using for target practice. But despite the pock marks she made out some stencilled letters on it, 'North And Maple'. With a beating heart she plunged on and the path began to widen and houses appear. Some had rusty mail-boxes at the roadside and in the dying light she made out names and occasionally numbers. When she saw how many of these lay ahead her spirits fell, but soon it became clear that there was nothing consecutive about them. A sudden lurch led her from twelve to twenty-six and soon after three figures loomed out of the dusk. She walked more slowly, her breathing constricted.

One hundred and eighteen was a ruinous mansion with boarded-up doors and windows and its neighbour little better, although inhabited. A name, Buster C. Howells, was painted on its mail-box. Peering closer she made out one hundred and twenty. She looked back at the ruin she had just passed and a hideous thought struck her. It had been lurking there deep down ready to strike ever since she had first found the address in her mother's old trunk, but she had kept it at bay until this moment. *Oh, dear God,* she cried inside herself, *don't let me have come all this way just for nothing.* With trembling hands she took out the piece of paper from her bag and held it up to the light but, of course, there was no mistake.

'Lookin' for somethin', lady?' The voice belonged to a young man with his hair in a ponytail who had slid out from under an old car she had taken for a wreck. He lay looking

57

up at her, a grin on his oily face.

'A hundred and nineteen,' she stammered.

He said, 'Sylvester?' and she said, 'Pardon?'

'You from Welfare?'

The irrelevance of the question nettled her; he saw it in her face. 'Old Sylvie. Lives up there in the trees. You're a week late, if you're from Welfare.' He pointed and she saw a wooded clump between the houses, a narrow beaten track like an animal-run leading towards it.

Without a backward look she set off, hearing his cruel young laugh follow her, until she reached the first of the trees. Nailed to the trunk was another mail-box with the name S. Vanderpool written on it. She felt faint and steadied herself against the rusty metal. *So close, so close.* Then, gathering her strength for the final push, she broke through the trees and stood staring at a caravan in a clearing.

It was long and sagged badly in the middle as if someone or something had jumped up and down gleefully for a long time on its curved aluminium roof. Each corner was supported by a pile of mossy bricks. There was no sign of life that she could see, its two windows had their curtains drawn tightly, but on a washing line was a pair of underpants, long and shapeless, of the sort that old men wear year in, year out. The sight of those faded old combinations moved her deeply for some reason and she stood a moment longer although she had ceased taking in any more of the scene, her eyes blind to the piles of bottles and tins and rusting motor parts that littered the clearing. Sylvester, she murmured, Sylvester Vanderpool, over and over again as if the name was reward enough for having come three thousand miles.

She walked back to her hotel in a daze, oblivious to the shades of night falling fast around her. On the porches cigarettes glowed like fireflies, reminding her of those childhood nights when she sat and watched the big beech tree, where the men sat out, darken until its outline merged with the night sky. Then she would return to her bed to dream of a man and a puppy and a little girl who was

58

herself. Sylvester Vanderpool, Sylvester Vanderpool.

The mood of high elation carried her through the streets of the town, past the lighted late-night shops and the winking beer signs, past the filling-station ablaze like a liner in the dark of the countryside, and finally through the glass doors of the Motor Lodge. She heard the sound of an electric organ coming from the bar and the clink of glass and the conversation of happy people. Happiness was welling up in her too, so she decided to go in and take her place among all these strangers. Her mood would automatically make her one of them.

At the bar she sat down on one of the stools and ordered the only drink she could recall from the films she had seen. She watched the young man in the short white jacket as he performed with the gleaming shaker in time to the electric organ. He grinned at her; she smiled back. Then he poured the glittering stream into a stemmed glass and added the olive on its stick with the same sense of fun. She put the glass to her lips and an icy arrow plunged straight down inside her, turning to fire the instant it found its target. Then, bursting, the heat spread to every part of her body. The sensation had similarities with that experienced earlier in her bath, only much more so, and when she looked at her reflection in the mirror behind the bar an even more attractive stranger than the one upstairs smiled shyly back.

She ordered another of the drinks and, chewing the pungent olive, allowed tiny selected fragments of what had happened to her so far to re-run in her mind. There were many questions to be answered and doubts to be resolved but the time for that would be later when she was lying at ease in her king-size bed upstairs. Queen-size, she thought to herself, and giggled, sipping gin.

A soft polite voice said, 'Good evening,' and in the mirror a well-dressed man in a light suit slid on to the stool at her side.

The barman asked, 'The usual, Mr Whiteside?'

The stranger sighed. 'My tastes never change. As you well know, Floyd.'

The young barman went off laughing. The man on the

next stool carefully laid a paperback book on the bar, then his cigarettes and a gold lighter on top to form a neat pyramid. His fingernails were scrupulously cared for and the lotion he was wearing had a musky Eastern aroma.

'Does smoking bother you?'

She said, 'No', in a quiet voice and they glanced at each other's reflection in the mirror behind the array of bottles. Then they were talking quite easily and comfortably as if it was the most natural thing in the world and when he asked her name and she told him he turned on his stool and stared at her with excitement on his face.

'Myrna Loy! It has to be. Tell me it just has to be!'

She laughed and said, yes, it was true, her mother had been a fan. Then he told her he was called Melvyn after Melvyn Douglas. She couldn't quite place the name but didn't admit to that, and his pleasure was so unfeigned and infectious that she allowed herself to be swept along with it. Then she had a closer look at his book on the bar as he was lighting a cigarette and her heart jumped. *Grand Hotel* by Vicki Baum. She had read every book this writer had ever written, every single one! Swivelling on her own stool, it was her turn now to look straight into the stranger's eyes.

He called out to the barman, 'Make that two of my specials, Floyd!' with a wave of his elegant hand, and when the glasses arrived, with their sugar-coated rims, she lifted hers to her lips and drank without a second thought.

Over dinner they continued to compare notes. It appeared they were in a similar line of business, at least, both of them sold things to the public. His stock in trade happened to be jewellery, nothing too precious, he laughed, mainly costume junk, Ciro pearls, that sort of thing. She thought of those two housewives she had talked to earlier and could well imagine the sort of thing that would appeal to them.

Then he said something that seemed out of character. 'I've been peddling trinkets to these shit-kickers for more years than I care to remember.'

In the middle of a laugh he stopped and apologised for

the expression and it was done with such charm that she thought no more about it.

'If I had a dime for every mile I've travelled over these old back roads, I'd have my own yacht by now. But, I don't suppose I'll ever see those far-off Aegean isles.'

He looked sad suddenly and she felt part of his sadness as though it were her own.

'My dear, dear daddy died when I was four. He was the last of the line. Old Augusta, Georgia, family. But then they say you don't miss what you've never had. More wine?'

She watched him fill her glass. The label said 'California Sparkling', above a picture of a smiling old man in a frock-coat holding up a bunch of grapes. For a moment some dislocation of perception had her convinced that it was the father he had been talking about. The organist was now playing a Glenn Miller medley and she wondered how much longer she would be able to hold herself in check for tonight everything, including the choice of music, conspired to have all her secrets tumble out of her. But, instead, some old caution made her say, 'Do you know anyone by the name of Vanderpool from these parts? Sylvester Vanderpool?'

He sipped his wine slowly.

'I know it's an unusual name.'

Her dinner partner looked at her. 'Unusual?'

She nodded.

'Not in this town, it ain't, honey. Half-Dutch, you know, that's where the name comes from. The other half's Indian. Red, not the other kind.'

He laughed loudly and she heard cruelty in its ring. Strange how a word like *honey* should have such a bitter sound to it. All the doubts she had kept locked up were now clamouring to escape. She thought of that rubbish-strewn clearing and the caravan with its wheel missing, but then she told herself that that man Rockford on the television lived in similar circumstances and what was wrong with the inside of *his* trailer? Nothing. She must learn not to judge these people and their country by the standards of her own part of the world. If she could only hold on to that, she told herself,

61

all would come right in the end.

'Myrna.' Playfully he reached out a hand to hers. 'Sounds like a song, don't you think? "Myrna From Smyrna"? I wonder if our friend over there could play it for us. He does requests, you know. You want to bet me?'

He laughed at her embarrassment and there was something very appealing in the sound. People around them seemed to think so as well, for quite a few turned and smiled in their direction and Myrna felt included in the general good humour aimed at their table. She thought of how they must look to these people, most of whom seemed to be locals dressed up for a night out. The men all wore business suits, none, of course, having the cut and colour of her partner's, while the women, in contrast, were decked out in lurid Lurex outfits that caught the light. They went in for a lot of jewellery as well, she could see that, which perhaps explained the popularity of the man facing her.

By this time a second old Californian gentleman had joined the first twinkling so happily at her from the wine bottle. She looked at the two of them side by side like two elderly brothers, so frisky for their combined ages and, not taking her eyes off either of them, she began to tell her story, past, present, and what she was hoping for in the future.

When she had finished Melvyn sat looking at the address which she had taken out of her bag to show him. He sighed. 'And some people say there's no romance left in this old world. Oh, Myrna, Myrna, what a truly *wonderful* story.'

This was more than she felt she could bear. Her eyes became moist, it seemed to her that never in her whole life had she been the recipient of so much affection and understanding. Suddenly this whole impulsive undertaking of hers seemed on the point of coming right: all the years she had nourished her dream had not been wasted after all.

In that same soft voice, he said, 'So he was a GI, you say, and you never ever saw him? Photograph?'

She shook her head.

'Makes it even more romantic. I must say, honey, you certainly don't look your age. You've got a real colleen's complexion.'

He was looking at her as though able to penetrate every secret part of her and her thighs trembled beneath the table, a strange and unfamiliar warmth located there. He ordered liqueurs and she drank the potent green syrup, although a tiny warning light had begun to glow dimly in the back of her brain.

After the second sticky glass things became hazy. She remembered seeing her face advancing and receding in a mirror, the sound of running water, the chill touch of tiles; most bizarre of all, a low fur-covered seat with a hole in the middle on which she sat for what seemed a very long time. Other impressions came and went, thrusting themselves at her like the reflection she had glimpsed earlier in that mirror. At one point all the people at the surrounding tables were looking and smiling at her while Melvyn seemed to be on his feet and telling them something. She felt it was about herself but couldn't quite make out what it was. The diners clapped, the organist played a chord on cue and then people were dancing. She may or may not have been on the tiny floor herself – she remembered feeling the smooth touch of Melvyn's lapels on her cheeks at one stage and the smell of his cologne – but that may have been later in her room...

She awoke next morning naked except for her brassière, her watch and a single earring. She was lying on top of the covers at an angle, head hanging over the edge of the bed as though she had fallen like that, remaining unconscious and unmoving until the moment her eyes opened on a scene of disorder and shame. The right-hand curtain of heavy blue velour had slipped or been torn from its pole, a chair was upturned and a drift of some white substance stretched across the carpet in an unbroken arc as though someone had tried to seed the deep pile by hand. Two empty bottles lay side by side in the midst of all this, but worse was the sight of her girdle, tights and pants draped playfully over the standard lamp which still burned, as did all the other lights. Her head felt as though it caged some ferocious beast; she didn't know how she was to get off the bed without enraging it further. But somehow she did so, crawling across the

63

carpet, leaving a trail in the talcum, until she would be able to reach the bathroom.

Half-way across she came face to face with a smiling, mouthing stranger. His handsome, greying head filled the whole of the television screen and, moaning, she reached forward to switch him off. Instead, his voice, backed by a heavenly choir, suddenly filled the room.

'Remember, dear friends, it is always better to walk with God than to ride with the Devil.'

She stabbed at the buttons in a panic and somehow managed to still the voice and shrink the smiling face to a searing blue dot.

So, it's a Sunday, she thought, and then it came to her that she must be suffering all those well known after-effects of the night before, just like the men she would see back home, moving about slow and miserable, on their day of rest. It was the first real thought to enter her head since she had opened her eyes, but before she could get back to the bed – the bathroom would have to wait – they were coming thick and fast in a vengeful swarm. Curled up under the sheets, thumb in mouth, she rocked with shame, remembering.

How could she have behaved that way, how could she? The question interrupted the rapid flow of images, then another horrid tableau; how could she have held him fast like that, after flaunting herself in that cheap, crude way, copied, it had to be, from some bad film. Oh God, she couldn't remember how far she'd been undressed before he finally made his escape. And the look on his face too, as he straightened his jacket.

'Honey, why kid ourselves, I wouldn't be any good to you, anyway. Believe me, you're really very sweet, but I've never gone all the way with any woman, even part of the way, if you must know. I'm just not made like that,' and the door closed.

To console herself she tried to recall some of the other things he'd said earlier, when they'd first come back to her room. He'd ordered more wine but it only made him sad.

Around his neck, he told her, was a reminder of his lost childhood. Oh, his mother was everything to him, she was still alive, very much so, in an old people's home in Florida, but she'd never been able to give him what he desired more than anything else in the whole wide world. He opened the locket to show her then, and she had leaned close to study the tiny faded photograph nestling among the dark hairs that sprouted in the opening of his silk shirt. They looked soft and inviting and she wanted to touch them; something that should have warned her about what was eventually to happen.

The man in the photograph wore his hair greased, with a parting in the middle, and had a heavy old-fashioned moustache. He looked more like a grandfather than a father, but Melvyn reminded her that he had been a late fruit from the tree, last of an already old line. There was a tear in his eye as he said it and she felt she could trust this man, so elegant in his tan suit and beautifully embroidered shirt. So she told him of that deeper, darker doubt that sometimes assailed her and he listened intently. It was then that he told her the story of the knife and the flower and the choice she would have to make when the time came for her to confront her past.

As though to remind her of the imminence of that moment, a vacuum-cleaner began roaring and bumping in the corridor outside. Her watch said eleven-thirty. According to the notice framed on the back of the door, that left her thirty minutes to pack and pull herself together. In the shower she turned the knob to cold and submitted herself to the chill needles for as long as she could bear, scrubbing, then towelling herself until she smarted and stung all over.

Outside the sun blazed down from a perfect blue sky and a stillness held sway, one she recognised. Sundays, it seemed, were the same everywhere. She heard singing, louder and more robust than she was used to, as she walked past a white-painted church, its car park full and glittering with shiny new metal. Tears came to her eyes and, with them, a

65

sense of deprivation. She should have been in there, she told herself, voice raised with all those others in their neat suits and spotless dresses, at her side that tall man of her childhood dreams, older and greyer, but with the same smiling dark eyes that she shared. She quickened her pace, heading with impatience now towards her destiny.

At the river she picked a flower, it might have been a weed here for all she knew, but it was purple and smelled sweet enough and would suit her purpose. She held it out in front of her as though it were a talisman to take her safely to her destination, past all those closed dark faces staring at her from their porches. Churchgoing didn't seem to have much appeal down here, and again she was reminded of the poorer part of her own town.

At the point where the road ran out, she turned into the narrow track, past the battered tin sign that read 'North And Maple'. The car outside the Howells man's house had gone and she felt relieved that this time she would be spared those mocking eyes following her as she pushed past and up to the trees ahead. The house itself looked deserted. And for a moment she stood in front of it, catching her breath, eyes fixed on the oil stain where the car had rested.

The story that had been told to her last night was something Melvyn had come across in one of his books, or it may have been told to him; that wasn't important. It was about someone like herself. This person, this woman, but it could just as well have been a man, had been asked the question – a flower or a knife, which would it be, which one would you want to give when the moment of confrontation arrived, which? She looked at the purple plant in her hand; it had begun to lose its freshness and scent in the noon heat. Her answer was there, so simple, so final, that she felt a great swelling of gratitude.

Myrna began to make her way, stumbling at times, up the narrow path at the side of the house, past the rusty mail-box with the name on it that should have been hers, until she reached the distant thicket of encircling trees. There was the trailer in its glade, curtains drawn as before, but this time a thread of smoke rose from the roof and, coming closer, she

66

saw that the clothes line had been stripped of its single item of washing. All she had to do was walk twenty yards over the littered, burnt grass and she would be travelling across thirty-nine years of her life. For a moment she thought of how she must look, certainly not at her best after last night and then, more importantly, what she would say. Her throat felt dry and unused. Not a word had passed her lips since all those things poured out of her in the small hours to a perfect stranger. As is often the case at such times, the phrase took on a startling aspect for no reason. How did two such words ever come to be yoked together in that way?

Holding out the flower, she cleared her throat experimentally and, as though she had triggered something off, the sound of an animal screeching broke out from inside the trailer, followed by a man's curses. The door burst open and a cat was hurled out, spitting and clawing. Myrna fell to her knees, gasping, as it came straight for her, back arched and tail stiff. Then the cat saw her and swerved with a howl, streaking off through the trees. She crouched there on the carpet of pine needles watching the open door, all her senses sharpened unbearably; the gum from the bark was making her head swim like an anaesthetic.

Then there was movement in the open doorway and a man filled the frame. A red plastic bowl was flung out and after it what looked like an old torn cushion, to join the rest of the rubbish scattered on the grass. An angry bellow broke from the man; it was directed at the trees where the animal had fled, but the crouching woman felt included in it. Then he stepped down on to the grass and she saw an old man in a plaid shirt many sizes too big for him and below its tail he was naked. Those ancient knotted shanks, dark as turkey meat, shocked and held her gaze. A long time, it seemed, passed before she could make her eyes travel up to his face, which was several shades darker and framed by lank locks almost to his shoulders. A strip of rag bound the low forehead and she wondered desperately what its effect reminded her of. The answer seemed terribly important for some reason.

She stared from her hiding place, hungry now for every

67

detail, and saw him send his eyes on a tour of the encircling woods. Then, lifting his shirt, he passed water before her very eyes. The watching woman closed them in horror but the sound, harsh in the silence and surprisingly vigorous for one so old, filled her ears and only seemed to compound the shame. The hissing ceased; she opened her eyes. He shook himself as men do and walked back into the trailer muttering and banging its door shut behind him.

The woman clung to the trunk of the nearest tree and tried to weep but found she could not. That long hair, the encircling headband; now she saw them for what they were, caste marks from the older side of the ancestry, the darker blood reasserting itself and, as she knelt there, it came to her that that same blood ran in her own veins as well. She saw herself suddenly, as though reflected in a mirror, naked; only this time there was no flattery, as there had been back in the hotel room. This time nothing could soften or disguise the reality of that coarse black triangle or the hue of her nipples, the unmistakeable tone of her skin. Old forgotten childhood taunts swam back, remembered agonies from school.

She stared down at the flower she had plucked earlier. Lying there, where it had fallen from her hand at the first moment of shock, it looked like a weed now. Slowly, she got to her feet and, not even noticing the pine needles clinging to her legs, she walked back down the path without a backward glance.

At the mail-box she halted. The name on its side meant nothing to her any more, for it had come to her that all her life up to this moment had been based on a lie, a lie that she had allowed to grow and flourish. She saw herself as she had been, aloof in her little glassed-in office high above the customers' heads and, at the window, that sad creature peering up at her. And then on the plane a glimpse of his double as though sent to remind her of the dangers for someone from her small world of following a dream to its conclusion.

She wondered where he was at this moment, the one the

town laughed at, wandering aimlessly along some country road back home along with all the other bored Sunday walkers. She saw him like that, scuffling along the grass verges, trailing a scattering of empty shells behind him as he went. Perhaps a trio of small boys further back throwing stones. The strange thing was, and it came to her not as a shock, but as something entirely reasonable, that that same shuffling creature in his heavy overcoat meant more to her than the man in the trailer she had travelled across a lifetime to meet. She had his blood, that stranger whose nakedness she'd seen, but she could just as easily have been the issue of the other, the one she had despised and mocked like everyone else in her town.

For the first time since she had started out that day she noticed the cry of the crickets, a bird with a strange liquid call and, in the distance, a train moaning like some wounded animal. She told herself she must leave this place, return to where she belonged. *Yes, Myrna, go back, go back home.* She was talking aloud to herself like some old woman with only her dreams to keep her company. But, of course, that was not the case any more.

From her handbag she took out the triangular scrap of paper that had started her out on this adventure and, opening the rusty flap of the mail-box, she laid it to rest inside among the dried leaves and old spider webs. Then she walked away down the path and back to the hotel where her single suitcase was waiting where she'd left it.

Bedroom Eyes

Standing at the microphone, left hand caressing the silvery stem, right casually hooked into the jacket pocket of his tuxedo – our hero. Yet another Saturday night compering the acts at the Four In Hand, leading to another damp twenty prised reluctantly from the till at the end of the night for his efforts and, in between, another night of no one, as yet, from down there offering to set up a drink. His mouth felt like the inside of God knows what, something parched and gritty anyway, but Ibbotson was adamant, as always: 'No drinking on the stand unless a customer buys it for you. And that's final.'

You were up there to work for *them*. *They* came to see sweat on your face; better still, spreading from the armpits. At some stage he always pulled his bow tie loose, an old un-favourite one, because he was particular about his clothes. But he no longer examined his jacket closely before hanging it up. He referred to it as his boiler-suit; and, indeed, wished it was, a baggy, soft one-piece with tin buttons and him inside it capering in his underwear like a man in a pantomime horse. Which was sometimes just the way he felt.

'This drunk man, you see... going home... *very* drunk... fell down in the gutter beside a pig... yes, a *pig*... puts his arm around the pig's neck... fast asleep... gets up in the morning... *horrified*... says, I had a feeling I'd made a mistake last night, the wife doesn't have as many buttons as that down the front of her nightie...' Wrong audience. Would have gone down a treat in some country hall back home, red agricultural faces splitting open at the familiar

70

image, heavy feet hammering the floorboards...

Mauve satin covering the hips in front of him now, a moulded bulge without cleft that wriggled past after his introduction. He placed a palm as if by gentle, fatherly accident on the thinly-covered Playtex while adjusting the mike with the other, maracas in hand, for she had chosen *The Girl From Ipanema.*

'... a young lady, folks, who is going places. And all you lovely people out there are about to launch another rising star because, *here, for the first time on any stage – tonight, for your entertainment – is...*' Name unimportant. Forgotten already.

This one couldn't sing to keep herself warm. But didn't know it. In the dressing-room she had been so drunk with her own dreams she hadn't even noticed he was making his customary pass at the new talent. He had even bent over her at one stage until two heads showed in the mirror and, unaware, she spat into her little make-up box and brushed on the moistened mascara. His fingertips crept slyly into vision around the soft pad of her upper arm, his cheek approached hers. Blue Grass, he guessed, with an underlay of nervous, oniony sweat... Denise, Dympna, Deirdre? 'Deirdre, darling,' he murmured, 'freckles have always been a great weakness of mine.'

She spat at the hollowed black cake in the tiny plastic box, this time missing.

'Shit!' she said, then, giggling, 'Oops, pardonny moi.'

A pat on the bare, warm shoulder to smooth his withdrawal and, 'You look gorgeous as it is, sweetie. No need to overdo it. Just listen for your intro after my spot. Okay?' But the sooty brush only continued thickening the lashes to geisha proportions as he closed the door behind him.

Matching suspender bumps breaking the racing descent of shiny satin from waist to hobbled ankles. Mermaid at the microphone. His patrons beyond the spotlight, husbands and wives with wedding anniversaries to announce,

71

courting couples, mixed doubles, drinking pals, girls from the office, lovers. But it was still one of those nights, sluggish, inert. Nobody loved him tonight. It could be like that, unpredictable, one time like this, the next they all wanted to pull you down off the stand across their laps and smack their great mothering chops all over you.

He would never fool himself for a minute that he was in the idol category – no one really wanted a lock of *his* hair – but he had had great red and purple transfers of mouths all over his shirt collars, and buttons had certainly popped, while the menfolk sat back making a great pretence of enjoying the spectacle.

The organ was taking the break now, its throb in the low register sending a not unpleasant shiver up the legs. But young Danny coaxed nothing out of the music. Within another twelve hours he would be wearing the same suit whilst playing hymns and church anthems, with identical dullness. He found it hard to forgive him sitting there each Saturday night putting such a magnificent animal through the paces of a poodle, for he had visions of himself on that furry stool, feet on the pedals, fingers busy with the keys and ivory stops, set on rape of the eardrums and bowels of the Saturday night crowd – his touch feather-light at first, then building to steel-rod jabs, loosening thighs, tickling a run of moisture, forcing moans, while the men sat poleaxed, brains pierced by an early, unbearable, dog-whistling note...

Someone was looking at him and not at the singer. Two of them, side by side. A blonde, a brunette. One much older than the other. Both wearing black leather. A touch of something a little removed from the natural, perhaps? Young pliable one under the spell of older woman from the office? *Men don't understand these things, dear. Shall I pin it up for you? How do you manage to keep it so soft?* So soft, oh so soft...

When the lights came up after the number he gave the younger one the eye, big, bad and bold. 'Oh, yes, there are certainly some lovely birds here with us tonight.' Would she giggle, blood in the cheeks, hot throb in the throat?

72

'Just as well I'm off the ladies for Lent...' He laughed along with the crowd. Felt handsome for a moment, showing his good Irish white teeth, shedding a few years.

'You know, ladies and gentlemen, it's very nice in our profession to get requests. It makes us feel that our work is truly appreciated. Isn't that right, lads?'

Old Cliff the drummer squeezed the bulb of his car horn in affirmation – the one used for novelty numbers. Easy come, easy go laughter from the crowd at the plastic-topped tables.

'But, in spite of all those requests, I'm *still* going to sing...'

A drunk at the back guffawed, but he might have been laughing at something one of his mates had said. Dimming of the lights, a few bars of soft intro from Danny to give him time to break the mike off at its narrow neck, and then down, thin, dark snake slithering after, among the tables and the upturned lit faces. *I'm in the m-o-o-d for l-ove, dear. Simply be-c-ause you're near me. Funny, but when you're near me, I'm in the m-o-o-d for l-ove...*

The vowels throbbed, he heard his own voice beating back at him and, deliberately, deepened the vibrato until the room pulsed. It made him smile as he crooned to the tables...

Later, in the taxi, speeding, arms around shoulders of breathing, moist leather – identical three-quarter lengths bought in a double shopping spree that very afternoon. Moments before his hands had been on silken knees slyly gauging differences in youth and flesh when the street-lamps ended and all was black behind the driver's neck, an upholstered cave with three bodies steadily heating its space.

Smells. Alcoholic breath, perfume, Fay's hair lacquer, his own aftershave but, overlording all, the steamy fumes from a tilted carrier bag in the corner by his feet. Three breasts of chicken with chips. Breasts... Knees... He closed his eyes, recalling that touch and the differing reactions – one, calm

73

acceptance, the other, a firm hand (he felt a cold-edged stone bite) removing his own, a breathed *tch tch* in his ear. His judgement seemed faulty for shouldn't acceptance, with that possible hint of compliance, have come from Fay and not the seventeen-year-old Madeleine?

He stroked the young cheek, gently screwing a finger into an ear. She jerked, giggled, and Fay, her mother – yes, her *mother* – leaned forward and laughed with her, squeezing the inside of his thigh. The two of them? Enough, he cautioned himself. Learn to take things as they come.

He relaxed with eyes closed and allowed the taxi to take him to destinations unknown.

One hour later. Young Madeleine's underthings were white froth and silk. The dark discs of her nipples showed clearly through the fine stretch of the garment that barely reached the top of her thighs. The little pink pants were a second skin showing her dark triangle coyly each time she moved. She was fresh, young and perfumed and her room was heaped with soft toys and costumed dolls from every European country. Marvellous, mouth-watering Madeleine...

Opening his eyes on cruder realities our hero could see a pair of much-washed Aertex undergarments over the back of a chair. Presently a soiled satin and elastic girdle joined them, the light went out, and a voice whispered with a giggle, 'Lazy bugger, where's your manners?' His fingers converged over a goose-pimpled back, found the shredded straps, fiddled briefly until there was a sagging looseness and a gust of relief. 'Now,' came the voice and, unaccountably, he sensed panic in himself: hadn't he done this countless times before? The bedclothes lifted, a weight of unfamiliar flesh searched out for and found him, a mouth fastened on his – moist suction cup – and he felt himself being kneaded energetically lower down between cold fingers.

But the image of the daughter still lingered. That time when she had tripped in to say goodnight, brushing his cheek with her lips, a conspiratorial laugh with her mother, then her rosy little buttocks flinching away and up the stairs to her own dreams of some pop star closer to her own age.

A mental sigh then – his mouth was still trapped wetly – and back to immediate responsibilities. But in mind, at least, he continued making love to that earlier image or, as the case might be, in other circumstances, in other beds, other forms – a limbo-ing mulatto; Heidi, in boots, who 'speaks four languages and breeds salukis for a hobby'; the girl in the Kodak ads; a bald shop-window dummy in a women's outsize shop...

His imagination working as he massaged, probed, then plumbed dutifully. The rhythm gradually becoming more frenzied, the breathing in his ear more of a whistle then, like an orchestral conductor, he brought the performance steadily and relentlessly to its climax. When she finally cried out he whispered, 'I love you,' with just enough passion – a gilding of the lily perhaps, but, no, rather the signature flourish of an acknowledged master in the field. His own pleasure followed then as a matter of course, a subdued tipping-over feeling that left him at peace and content. The disordered bed seemed to float a little as he twined fingers with gentle possessiveness in her damp bush; his eyes closed.

Then, out of the darkness, she said, 'Give us a cigarette,' and the tone of voice was all wrong. He hesitated before replying, 'I don't smoke,' and she said, 'I might have guessed.'

Experimentally he squeezed her tangled mound but she rolled away from his touch with a grunt. He heard her fumbling among the clutter on the night table. Something heavy fell to the floor with a thud, then a tinkle. He heard her swearing to herself. Then she found what she sought and his eyelids contracted just a little too late before the match flared. Why did they all have to smoke *afterwards?*

She was lying beside him on her back, puffing, arms bare to the shoulders.

'Why did you say that?' she said.

Again the tone of voice was wrong. 'You didn't have to, you know.' They lay side by side, silent, and the swelling tick of the alarm-clock where it had fallen on the floor mocked him. If he'd reacted quickly – a superior laugh that said, oh, come on now, we're two grown-up people and we know, don't we, words like that are part of the game – but he hadn't, and now he would have to get out of it in the only way left open to him.

His clothes came easily to him in the dark: he had piled them out of long habit by the foot of the bed. She didn't even say, 'Where are you going?' but lay invisible, complacent trunk and legs buried under the bedclothes, only her cigarette tip signalling her position.

Did she laugh softly then as, next instant, the bedside light came on and found him hopping on one leg into his shorts? He felt conscious of his legs, thin, hairy and bald on the calves, a blue vein or two. His face should have been pale but he knew it was inflamed as he tugged and buttoned. Back turned to the bed now as he bent in front of the dressing-table mirror. He found himself whispering to the flushed face in the glass – *right over left twice, up and under,* as if he had forgotten how to knot a tie. There was a framed photograph of a petty officer on the smeared table-top among the brushes and cream jars – tilted face, moustache, smiling eyes that had watched all of their antics.

She said, 'The great lover has had his pride hurt. Mr Bedroom Eyes.' He said nothing. He was still having trouble with his stinking tie and wanted to be dressed and clear before she started to shout.

Then she laughed and he knew then that she would never raise her voice. Why should she? 'You all think you've got something special between your legs, don't you? And, like that other grinning bastard over there, most of you would put it where I wouldn't put the tip of my umbrella...'

Hurriedly he slid on his shoes, doubling the leather under one heel. Stooping to prise it free, he felt dizziness. His palm steadied him for a moment on the carpet, then he headed for the door. He wouldn't even give her the satisfaction of a goodnight, the cow!

He twisted the knob, pulled, but the door held. He heard

her laugh. 'Okay, okay,' he said, 'where's the bloody key? Where is it?'

She continued laughing and, turning, he saw her thick neck bared, head back among the pillows, the rest of her hidden, shaking under the slithery eiderdown, the way it was in the films, stock situation terminating in a pair of hands – his – squeezing, squeezing... Why couldn't she see it that way, realise her peril? But, more important, why couldn't he simply go over, a smile on his face, take her by the throat, not savagely, mind you, and shake her a little, barely bruising the flesh. Just, for once, doing something instinctively...

He crossed to the dressing-table and began moving tubes, jars, hair-clips and knotted elastic bands about on the glass surface, stirring fresh patterns in the dust.

'Isn't it there?' she asked.

'No!'

'Then we're both locked in.' More laughter and the bed shook. He could feel it across the room, a soft yet powerful rumble he imagined penetrating the very structure of the house. The petty officer still regarded him, smiling, his eyes fixed on his like one of those poster faces that possess one the length of the street, and sometimes even beyond.

Where Are You Taking Us Today, Daddy?

A question I had come to dread each Wednesday afternoon with my two children – the boy, a sturdy human projectile aimed at all around him, and his sister, older, more distraught, given to frenzies that eased off into rapid thumb-sucking. It was she who always asked the question and my disquiet owed more to the reminder stirred in me that I had deserted them and their mother, and that these weekly outings constituted a poor attempt at penance, than to any reproach of my inventiveness. Her fine little limbs, her thin blonde plaits, one of which invariably broke loose in a rush of baby hair, her small face – at a distance its dwindling could squeeze me cruelly – these were my punishments. So, on this sunny day I had laid my plans carefully in advance. When they clambered into the car after school their eyes fell on the propped long canes with their muslin nets, and the two gleaming jam-jars.

'Oh, *I* know where we're going. We're going fishing!' my daughter called out and her brother echoed, 'Going *fishing*, going *fishing!*' Despite his independent rumbustiousness, he always followed in her wake, imitating after a slowly dawning moment each of her inventions, no matter how outrageous, then taking it up with such seriousness that it became his alone until he would begin to realise once more that she had moved on to something new, and so once again the cycle repeated itself. I often wondered if the habit would continue as he grew older and now, as I drove, I watched him fumble, eyes clouding, as his sister hurtled through a series of questions, how, when, where, why, with no concern for an answer. I had a fellow feeling for my son.

'Daddy, are we nearly there yet?' asked my daughter.

Before my son had time to shape his echo, I said, 'Yes, sweetheart, almost there,' and it was quite true this time.

I steered the car between two grey, leprous pillars, pointed, in the fashion of the country, to cheat the fairies of a dancing platform (had I ever told them of the custom? it might prove a useful diversion on the way home) and at once felt a slide of memories begin. This green tunnel, its growing walls encroaching steadily as the car bumped forward – where was it leading me after all these years? I felt proud of its rare decay, so that when my daughter asked in a small wondering voice, 'Daddy, are you sure this takes us to the seaside?' I smiled, not answering, full of my double secret.

There behind those banks was the no-man's land we had made our domain, a small triangle waist-high in briar and grasses that grew thicker each spring. Tracked constantly by our feet and blackened by our fires, it held more intimacy than a bedroom. Our archaeology had been random but we certainly must have unearthed every coin, marble, shard of coloured glass, crockery, clay pipe and metal that lay among the roots or under them. Our gaze at life then seemed to be a downward one. And our imagination fed too on the more modern detritus that we found there, condoms, scraps of underwear, mystifying bloodstained pads.

Now we were passing the mouth of a lane barred by two rusty bed-ends. I had slept between ends like those as a child, the tips of my fingers on the wheel transferring momentarily to those black enamelled joints, so many to explore in the dark. Beyond the barrier, a churned up expanse of mud. Cattle must be fed or rather watered there. Lurking somewhere in the shadow of the hedge would be an old plugged bath, tide-marked with slime, iron claws deep in soft blue muck. I couldn't remember such a thing, it must be recent, and the look of the place told me clearly that no one lived in the big old house any more.

We would go there for eggs and buttermilk, always in twos, never alone, for the brothers had the look and smell (that last we guessed) of characters in a horror film. One had a crooked back but, despite his angled body, always climbed the ladder into the hayloft to bring down the still warm eggs in his cap while his brother sat in the huge gloomy kitchen staring at the wall in front of him. Neither of them ever spoke to us. A hand, like a charred stick, would be held out for our money and would close and remain clenched, suspiciously, until we had backed out of the kitchen and run down the lane, the buttermilk storming in the can.

I laughed out loud remembering all that.

'Daddy,' came the small female voice from the back seat, 'what are you laughing at?'

'Oh, nothing, love. When I was your age I used to live here.'

'Where was your house, Daddy? Is it near here?'

'We'll see it very soon, if you're patient.'

'Did you live at the seaside, Daddy?'

'No, pet, the sea's very far from here.'

'But I thought we were going fishing today.'

'So we are, love, so we are.'

The car bumped on. It was obvious no other wheeled traffic ever ventured down this way. I wondered how the local inhabitants, if there were any left, managed for bread, milk, groceries – the regular daily or twice-a-week supplies which used to come in tradesmen's vans, a grandiose term for Jimmy Mill's old horse and cart with its weighing machine on a flat herring box, or the breadman's red and cream van with those deep drawers that pulled out to an impossible, sagging length.

'I have a surprise for you.'

'We're going out in a *boat!*'

'No, there are no boats here.'

'We're having a *picnic!*'

'No picnic.' (Sadly.)

'We're going to see granny?'

'Granny doesn't live here. She lives in town.'

Weakly I fended them off for in truth the magician's sleeve was empty. I was a sham. I had no surprise and I certainly hadn't the necessary genius to invent one at this late stage. Why had I ever said it?

'This is where Daddy played as a boy.'

I had slowed the car out of deference to this monument from my youth. 'Well?' I said, turning to them. 'Well?'

The girl looked at me.

'Well, would *you* like to live here and play here?'

Silence.

'It's awfully dirty. And all the windows are broken. Do gipsies live here?'

I laughed. Then I stopped the car and, with the engine running, looked up at the building filling the sky. Its ugliness and sheer size seemed all the more savage because of its surroundings – green fields, hedges, trees, a glint of slow river in the distance; the incongruity of this brick and stone behemoth planted brutally in the countryside. When I was a child, of course, I accepted it and its place completely. My friends lived in this tenement block, because it was inhabited, and so densely that outside a careful radius it was known as the 'Breeding Cage'. Officially and to the people who lived in its two storeys its name was Summerhill, a name at laughable variance with its tiny dark apartments, its rusty iron gangway half-way up and running the length of its blank rear wall, the dark alleyway in its shadow, the row of dry closets. But looking at it now and with my daughter's observations in my ears, I saw it as it really was on this summer afternoon, an ugly, decaying monster.

I eased the car past over pot-holes and flattened mounds of clinker, my last backward glimpse that of the beech tree still standing in what were once neat allotments and now was a rank weedy jungle. There was a seat encircling its thick initialled trunk and I remembered how the men would wait there in the summer dusk for the racing pigeons to arrive from railway terminals with foreign names like Crewe, Fishguard, Wrexham.

'Daddy, were you *very* poor when you were young?'

'Not terribly poor, no.'

We had reached the end of the rutted track. It swung on

over the old wooden bridge but planks were missing and it was obvious no vehicle had crossed this part of the river in a very long time. The children had got out and were running about with excitement at their release in the soft air. It was certainly peaceful – birds, river sounds, a distant buzz from the far-off arterial road, but when I looked at the bridge I feared the day was ruined because, even if the way were passable, how could I convey my two reckless town children over those gaping holes?

'Now,' I said, 'we're going to cross this old bridge, but you must hold my hand very tight. Do you understand?'

The boy surged forward instantly and I called his name in a panic. At the first rail of the bridge he stopped to stare back at me, slyly, I thought. His sister glanced between the two of us. 'I don't want to go across that bridge. It's too dangerous.'

'Don't be silly!' I shouted. 'There's nothing to be afraid of, if you take my hand.'

Then, 'Now, is there?' – an attempt at cajolery after the devastation of that roar on the country peace. I looked back at the great pierced bulk of brick and stone. There was no sign that I had aroused any flicker of life there; only the starred mirrors of glass in the black face reflecting the sun.

'Give me your hands,' I said, pulling them into position on either side of me. 'It's like hopscotch, you see, you miss the spaces and walk on the wood.'

The boy entered the game willingly, but his sister's captive hand twisted and dragged in mine. 'You're not going to let your brother beat you now, are you?' I whispered. 'It's only an old bridge, after all.'

'I don't care, I don't care,' she cried. 'You shouldn't have brought us here. Mammy *never* allows us to go near water.'

'Very well, then. We'll just stay here – on this side of the bridge – and not go fishing either.'

The boy's howl would have melted a heart of stone but, unrepentant, his sister only tossed her pigtails, moving away to a clump of yellow daisies that grew on the river bank. I lay back among the grass and, for the first time that day, had a moment of peace. The feeling came from my protected position, the shallow grave I had formed for myself among the standing, growing things. They outlined my body, waving gently back and forth, touching face and hands.

I was remembering another hollow, the depth of a bath, we used to play in. Its beautiful stamped-out symmetry lay unexpectedly in the middle of a dip between the parallels of river and mill-race. The grass covering its sides and floor was fine, springy, with an almost carpet-like pile. In an afternoon we might transform our hollow from a bus to a lifeboat, Flying Scotsman to a racing eight. At Easter we picnicked in that place, cracking dyed eggs; in May we conducted our queen there in trailing yards of old lace curtain, head garlanded, hand in hand with her black-faced consort. I remembered battles, indignities, sexual experiment, all enacted in that rectangular cockpit. I would certainly have to see it again.

The distant yelling had died by this time to a murmur that sounded like reconciliation, both heads bent now over the daisy clump. Raising myself from that bruised outline in the grass, I went across to join them. '*I* know where there are some poppies,' I said. Fragile, slithery petals of moist red silk waving in the grass beside the upper mill-race, that dark deep ribbon that once swallowed a runaway pram while its young keeper screamed helplessly from the bank high above...

'Where?'

'Oh, just over the bridge. Up there.'

I pointed to where the track climbed up and over another bridge, the one we called the Iron Bridge because of its twin girders slung low over the smooth silent rush.

'It's up to you,' I said, glancing away from her. What complexity there was inside that small blonde head with its neat slicing divide.

'Come on,' she shouted to her brother, and together they raced to the bridge. At the very edge she halted him adroitly to stare back at me. My heart pumped as I went up to them. We looked at one another. If I didn't understand my daughter and her ways, she certainly seemed to see all of mine for what they were.

Hand in hand we crossed the bridge. The river swam below, dim green through the spaces where the planks had been torn up or had rotted away to leave ragged fragments clenched about the nails. Weed streamed like water-borne hair straight and taut with the current. When the level fell it lost its vigour, collapsing into foul-smelling brown masses over the stones. It was always a fearful experience to lift a corner of that matted curtain with a stick to disclose the scuttling horrors underneath. I tried now to pierce the rippling green sheets to where rusty bicycle wheels, jagged bottle ends, tin cans lay anchored. Did children still forage in these low reaches? I thought selfishly of that water lying untouched, unsearched, since I myself had waded there.

We left the bridge and now our feet fell on hard-packed cinders. By the side of the path wild rhubarb grew – I remembered those too – broad leaves, elephant ears, fluted green stalks.

'No, don't touch,' I cautioned, adding the easy lie that always seemed to work – 'they're poison.'

We passed and I almost relented when I saw their yearning looks. What harm could a couple of waving green parasols do? But then I remembered the bitter clinging smell of the sap and how, as children, we learned never to go near the plants with our hands.

I looked at the two of them ahead of me now, the girl jigging frantically in that restless way she has, her brother bouncing lovingly in her wake. My children, with my blood, my characteristics. I had denied myself one of the great joys when I had left home, for in one afternoon a week how could I possibly discern even a single inherited trait?

Catching up with them, they were examining a dead bird at the edge of the path, I said, 'Well, wouldn't you like to live here?'

'Not really,' said my daughter – then, 'Daddy, what did this bird die of?'

'Chicken-pox?'

'Oh, Daddy, you *are* daft,' she cried, beating my bulk with her tiny fists while her brother raced about us in an ecstasy. Lifting her under the armpits I swung her up then around in a circle, her heels rising gradually from the ground to whirl out straight and weighted in the air.

'*Me too, me too,*' yelled the boy so, after I had dumped her giggling in the grass, he too, willing centrifuge, was whirled through the air. Then we collapsed to lie beside her, all three of us among the dry crushed grasses. My ears were singing and the blue cloudless sky shifted drunkenly very high above.

'When I was your age ...' I said, for they both lay at peace now, two hay-field babes from an English painting, 'we used to –' I thought of the possible effect of what I was about to tell them – 'we used to light little fires here.'

Holding each of their hands, I continued, 'We would light that bank over there when the grass was dry. You see how it hangs over like a curtain? One of us would put a match to it, then the rest would light their bunches of dry grass from that.'

I wondered if the image would move in my girl's mind – the brightening puffs of flame as each dried tuft in the chain was ignited, the crackling, the smell, the heat on the cheeks, the race from red bursting tussock to the next. All of us working along the bank, our own patterns of arson fixed firm in our minds. God knows why we did it, but once the lust rose in us we would have kept on until we had blackened the entire landscape or until we dropped. And the madness lasted throughout those late summer and early autumn weeks when growth had stopped and was turning to tinder.

The older boys in the village followed their own more dangerous variant by setting fire to the whins near the railway line. Everything seemed magnified to our senses, the fierce heat, the tracer bursts of sparks, the smoke, as we stood at a distance, barred from that excitement. Hares and nesting birds would explode from under our feet, their pursuit draining away some of the frustration. And afterwards, that reeking waste, ugly, piebald but, worst of all, those depressing fragments exposed for all the world to see – single old boots, cracked bottles, tins, nameless metal parts – a whole year to hide all that from sight once again.

'Daddy, I want to go fishing.' The boy's voice came as a soft rebuke.

'Fishing it is, then,' I countered briskly. 'No more dawdling, and a prize to whoever gets first catch.'

The boy howled suddenly. 'We've left the nets behind!'

'They're in the car,' I said. 'I'll go get them, but you must stay here, not move from this spot. Promise?'

The boy nodded, a docile believer. His sister had a look in her eye I felt it better to ignore, but what could I do? On days such as this I would wish almost anything to keep the peace between us.

At the bridge I turned to wave jauntily, an excuse to check on their safety. My God! That deep, dark current mere yards away, the colour of a gun-barrel and twice as dangerous; pools in the stream behind, shallow certainly, but deep enough to drown a stumbler; I'd left them surrounded by dangers. I have nightmares in which the recurring horror is their joint deaths – by electrocution in the home, a bathroom drowning or by sudden collision when, hand in hand, they wander innocently out from behind a parked ice-cream van. That warning carillon can freeze the blood in the middle of a street in broad daylight.

I crossed the bridge and got to the car, controlling my panic. From the floor I quickly picked up the thin canes with their crumpled nets and then the two jam-jars. Turning to go back with both arms full, my travelling gaze took in a dreadful sight. The girl was lying on her stomach on the far bridge, head down over the water, holding something in the flow. The boy crouched a few feet away watching her.

For some reason I started to count in my head. At all costs I must not force her into any sudden action. Fourteen, fifteen, sixteen – all the while my eyes burning up that distance between – seventeen, eighteen, nineteen. On the silent beat of twenty-two the boy stood up and moved a little

86

way to meet me. He was confused, I could see that. She said something to him, something I couldn't hear, and he laughed and skipped in the air.

The final yards – thirty-six, thirty-seven, I counted – were taken at increasing speed for I feared some last minute treachery. Then I was on the bridge looking down at her. The long stalk in her hand pulled strongly in the current. She watched it with absorption, elbows a mere foot from the sinister rush.

'Didn't I tell you not to come up here?' I held my voice steady. Dear God, such control.

She continued to stare down at her drowning flower and the vee it formed in the current.

'Well?'

I brought one of the canes down on the backs of her uncovered thighs. Although I was incensed, the blow, I felt, still had a force carefully strung between playfulness and severity. A faint line of colour appeared on the legs below me but she persisted with her experiment with the flower and the water, ignoring me still. My anger grew righteous. Strong phrases I'd heard my own parents use clanged in my brain. I yanked her up by one arm, pulling the dripping stalk from her hand, then hurled it far out into the fast dark stream.

'Now,' I said. 'We came here to fish and we're *bloody* well going to fish.'

Her brother took the jam-jars and canes wonderingly when they were thrust into his arms. I began dragging her across the bridge. There was a crash behind us. I turned to see the boy looking down at the glittering remains of one of the jars at his feet.

'Okay, okay,' I said, 'forget it. We'll put all the fish in one jar. Now, let's go.'

But, once off the bridge and back on the hard-packed path again, she started to yell, 'I want to go home, I want to go home.' And then – 'I want Mammy.' Oh, that knifing thrust.

Clamping her wrist, I raced her feet over the ground.

Then she stumbled, falling on her knees, and all resolve drained away as I stood over her, checked by an image of tender young skin stippled black with cinders. The temptation to let her have her victory and walk away, as I had done earlier, was a strong one.

So how then did it come about, seconds later, that I was jogging along the river path holding my daughter under one arm like a sagging roll of carpet? The impulse had come suddenly, a momentary madness. As my knees wobbled and my heart pumped I thought of the sight presented to someone who might be watching at a distance, this grown man bumping along with his human burden, both shouting, and the small harassed boy trotting along in their wake. One of those curious dream-like memories to haunt and puzzle, even years later.

But of course the pantomime had to come to an end, and eventually the limp, sobbing figure was allowed to slip from my grip on to the grass at the edge of the path. I bent over her, panting, while she thrashed on the ground, her brother watching from a distance. I thought of a pact between the two of us, the boy and the man, a couple of males against this ultimate terrifying show of feminine obduracy.

I took the nets and the remaining jam-jar from his hands. 'Well,' I said, '*I'm* going fishing, at any rate. If you want to come with me, that's perfectly all right. If not – please yourself,' and walked off down the path. The track, rutted by winter flooding, dipped sharply down and at right angles past the old mill, a smaller version of the building across the river. I had now passed out of sight and a momentary twinge came at me. I waited for a moment, hidden, then peered around a peeling gable end. The boy was stranded in his own no-man's land half-way along the path between his sister, still kicking her heels in a tantrum, and myself. The fact registered almost thrillingly. *He had followed me.* That he was becalmed and could quite easily be wooed back to that furious presence among the grass seemed unimportant.

I turned a familiar corner – the house I'd once lived in with my parents and younger brother was an end house –

and came out into the open space before the row. As I had anticipated, no one seemed to be living in the cluster of houses any more. Windows had been carelessly boarded up, doorways filled with sheets of corrugated tin. I remembered the people who had occupied these dwellings, faces, names, the individual aura of each and every one, their dress, habits, way of speaking.

Our old house was now used as a storehouse for animal feed. The door had been taken from its hinges. Sacks were propped up in the dark interior of what used to be the big room where the black kitchen range had burned. For a moment I felt upset at the uncaring way strangers had used what was to me the central structure of my early life. I sent my gaze along the rest of the row, each house with its hooped water-butt, now green with neglect, sunk a few inches in the dirt beside the front door.

Smoke was rising from the chimney of the last house. Could the Quigleys still be here? They were a large male family of violent and coarsely backward ways. I remember the boys used to have their hair cut round the rim of a bowl which, with their flat features, gave them an Amazonian head-hunter appearance. They were sensitive to ridicule and lived close to the hearth. No one in the village had ever been allowed into their house, which lent it a mystery of dark, unspeakable rarity. The mother, too, was rarely seen. It was rumoured she sat beside the fire all day long, a huge overblown creature wearing a pair of men's outsize plimsolls on her swollen feet. This image of her sitting squaw-like in the dark smoky interior of the furthest house always conjured up for me the theory that the Quigleys really did have Redskin blood, a family of racial changelings. And the boys' passion for fishing, shooting and caged animal-life added further weight – they'd had an encampment of hutches and shanties at the bottom of their garden which always seemed to be their true home.

A kennelled dog began barking. The sound came from that very spot. Then, incredibly, old Ma Quigley herself appeared in her doorway, a hand shielding her eyes from the sun. She saw me and stared and I nodded an apologetic greeting before moving off down through the allotments. I was hoping for a path, one I remembered, but all was overgrown now and I had to stumble on, embarrassed, through plants once domestic but now fierce and unrecognisable. Although I didn't turn my head I was certain I was still being observed. Once I almost fell full length. Any moment now a piercing voice would bellow out that I was trespassing. But no sound came and when finally I clambered up and out of the wilderness, trouser legs thick with burrs and flecked with cuckoo-spit, and glanced around, the old woman had vanished. The house-fronts were as lifeless as before. Only that thin line of rising smoke was there to remind me that I hadn't imagined that forbidding figure, for, as their ages increased, so also had the Quigleys' terror for me as a child.

And then I had a pang of conscience about my own children. The same emotions I was remembering might very well be paralysing them at this very moment.

I stood on the raised narrow path packed hard with grit. Nearby, a length of rusted cable barred the opening to the river and the trickling weir. I waited anxiously for a sight of them, my eyes fastened on the gable end of our old house. They must appear there if they were following me. What else could they do but be drawn this way? They wouldn't go back without me, not across the wooden bridge, not across those dark gaps in the planks widening between their legs. I waited. But then, of course, there was a wilfulness in all children, wasn't there?

The thought of a double drowning, or, just as bad, limbs bent and broken! I saw myself discovering them, racing for help, yet wanting to stay, my indecision reducing their chances. I began the numbered count out loud this time. At fifty-five the boy came into sight around the edge of our house wall. I stopped counting. He hadn't seen me yet. He was blinking into the sun which had burst out above and behind me and was flooding the row of old peeling houses with a harsh, unfriendly light.

90

I wanted suddenly to be dabbling in the pools and under the stones where the water purred and trickled invitingly. I leaped up and waved the nets in the air in frantic semaphore. Now he had seen me. I heard his shout and quickly dropped from sight. The game had begun.

He disappeared to return a moment later dragging his sister by the hand. He kept tugging and pointing. What a passionate go-between he was, working on her 'now tirelessly. I loved him. Of course I loved her, too. But she needed more, didn't she? I watched to see which of them would find my tracks first. The girl's imagination would probably not be as sympathetic as his to the idea of a game of Red Indians. And I was right, for he fell upon the trail straightaway, like a terrier, while she made off haughtily at right angles towards the raised path on which I crouched. Now he was looking after her, uncertain. For a moment, God forgive me, I prayed for her to come to grief as she beat a path through the dense growth, to be forced back to the start of that wriggling hypotenuse I had laid down, but she continued to surge forward while he ploughed on along his own course, dispiritedly now.

I could see that the girl was going to reach me first. She was striding contemptuously along the path, her sandals striking its baked surface. Down below, his head on a level with her feet, the boy puffed and lurched among the weeds. He kept falling over hidden humps and into trenches. Insects were rising about his hot face and arms. I felt I had failed him. He looked ready to cry at any moment so I stood up in full view before ducking under the wire and into the place beside the water.

The place hadn't changed. It was still untouched, although the grass looked as though it had been recently swept, for there were no droppings, no hoof-prints, only a delicate line of white drift edging the bank. It was still magical. I touched the turf and sniffed the rank river-water smell.

The girl appeared. She showed no embarrassment, moving past me as though I wasn't there. I watched her

91

throw pebbles into the deeper reaches of the river. She was the prize all right, cool and inaccessible, standing there, feet apart, her tiny hand coming up each time above her shoulder. The smooth-washed stones flew then plopped in the water. Their ripples lapped against the top of the weir staining the wood. The planking there looked porous, bleached white with repeated wettings then drying out through long, hot afternoons. The sun was such a cleansing thing. I would dip my bare arm into the water, then feel it prickling in that fierce heat, and smell the fierce muddy odour. Fresh water always had a pull for me the sea could never have.

'Daddy, I'm here.'

Proud words of an Indian scout who had made it against overwhelming odds. He stood before me, sweating, knees scratched, a streak of dirt on one cheek, waiting for orders but praise as well.

'Good man,' I said. '*You* came the hardest way.'

Was that a sneer on his sister's face? A stone flew with distinctly better aim. The boy looked after it with envy, then at the spreading rings on the water.

'And now,' I said quickly, 'let's fill that jar you've got with lots of fish to take home to Mammy.'

It was a foolish thing to say, but I reckoned I would have him once the first catch of the day wriggled inside his net. I would teach him to love my river as I did.

'They're hiding under the stones,' I whispered. 'We must tickle them out.'

'Tickle,' he repeated, savouring the word.

I began lifting stones, clouding the water. He began to prise and lever with me. We kept moving on to fresh pools. When all seemed lost we came upon a solitary minnow, steady in the water, fins beating, pop-eyes staring straight ahead at nothing, female. A fine thread floated from its red bursting belly. The net glided forward. The fish held itself above the bed of the stream as if drugged by the sensation of water on its sides. I knew we had it but felt disappointment that the first catch was to be this dulled creature close to

92

death. At the last moment I put the cane into my son's hands and he followed through, a little jerkily, but he took his fish. I showed him how to keep the bottom of the net with the catch in it just under the surface of the water, while I went off for the jam-jar.

His sister was still busily pelting the surface of the river. 'Why don't you come and help your brother?' I said. She snorted, 'There's only one jar,' but I sensed weakening.

Without saying any more, I picked up the jar and went back to the pool. Clumsily, the boy and I, we manoeuvred our stickleback out of the mesh and into the cloudy water in the jar. No magic occurred, only the crazed bumping of a fish-mouth against glass walls. I felt we had damaged that swollen body terribly in some way. We busied ourselves with netting another, and as we went about the task I kept up a commentary aimed secretly at the girl.

'No, don't put the net in like that, you'll only scare them away. Slide it in, that's right, then leave it ready for them when they put their heads out. It's not easy, you know. Not many people *can* catch spricks . . .'

I noticed that the stoning had ceased, the birdsong and sound of the stream no longer punctuated by slapping explosions. Then I saw her going casually across to the other net that lay on the grass, touching it with her foot, moving it a little with studied boredom. In a loud whisper I said to the boy, 'Look, did you see that big one going into the tin-can?' A lie, but soon she too was bent over one of the pools we had left, net in hand, probing softly.

And now the afternoon was drawing to a close, the light tightening around us, the three of us intent among the submerged stones and all the other anchored objects, learning cunning as we went. A feeling of contest was in the air.

Then the girl caught one. She held up her net in panicky delight. 'Look what I've caught! Look! *Look!*'

I made a point of keeping my head down over the water, holding the small hands on the cane in mine with a firmer grip. The boy wanted to go to her aid. I never wanted him to grow out of that innocence. A little animal, the heat from his round red face rising into mine, his hair soaked with sweat, fingers slippery on the thin bamboo.

'There's only one jar,' I said. To the boy – 'Do you mind another fish in with yours?'

He thought deeply for a moment. 'Will they fight?'

'Well...'

'Oh Daddy, please hurry up or my one will die!'

'Hang on,' I called.

She shook her catch impatiently in with the other one and I waited to see her face when the two goggled snouts would push at her suddenly through the glass. But she pulled the net away quickly, rushing back to the water.

I examined the captives myself, two staring torpedoes, now held to the glass by their sucker-like lips, then switching away to pose hypnotized at a new angle. The newcomer was fierce, herding the fat female savagely around the circular wall, her presence an obvious irritation to him.

At the foot of a bank I placed the jar carefully upright, then sat down myself, sinking into a cushion of springy grass. Larks sang somewhere out of sight; the two children were intent and silent. Soon they would join forces, perhaps fight, then end up beating the water, then each other, with the nets. I would have to intervene, conciliate, then round them up before taking them back to the car and home. And the girl would say, 'Daddy, where are you taking us next week?' But now the sun lay on my closed eyelids and by stretching out I could just touch the circle of calm water in the jar and wait for that first delicate exploratory nibble on my fingertip. For the moment at least, it was as if I was back to an earlier age and my children never existed.

Happy Hours

Each morning after breakfast they set out for the beach across the dusty stretch of no-man's land just outside the hotel. It was where the waiters played football with furious energy during the siesta, greatly to the surprise of the English tourists who had come expecting the traditional afternoon lull, but, at this time of day, only the town dogs patrolled the expanse. Reno was nervous of the strays, skirting them warily, on the lookout for the tell-tale white scum around the muzzle, but the other two only laughed at him and his anxiety. By this time they were familiar with such phobias, brought about, so Thurso was convinced, by all that reading behind bars. He and Peebles, perhaps because of a common professional interest, were more taken by the story they had heard about the Civil Guard on the streets after nightfall shooting anything canine that moved in the light of their headlamps.

The yellow dust rose then eddied about their ankles as they headed for the short run of skyline between the Barbados and the Antigua. They crossed the road, past the bus-stop where there was already a queue for Palma, men, women and children in shorts with reddened faces, holding carrier bags. Some of these bore the imprint of the Union Jack, but Thurso and Peebles experienced no fellow-feeling, disaffection having set in on the plane from Gatwick, and Reno, sly Reno, grinned to himself each time he noticed their distaste. He hugged his secret delight even now as a man in the bus queue began to complain loudly and bitterly to his neighbour about something in his day-old *Express* concerning the Falklands business. But the other two gave no indication they had heard and moved into the shadows.

At the end of the alleyway the sea was a band of blue running waist-high between the walls of the two hotels. It hadn't changed colour since the day they first sighted it from their coach, the identical postcard tint they had somehow always imagined it to be. Almost everything was the way they had expected it would be, only the smells were new and unsettling. People left their garbage in the streets quite openly here and it was best not to think of just how far the sewage was pumped out into the bay before it started on its lazy return.

The concrete of the alley ended abruptly and they dropped down into soft grey sand. Reno stopped to unlace his training shoes but the other two ploughed on, determined not to let the shifting drifts beat them. It was a ritual that never varied; while Reno, barefoot, followed at his leisure with a grin on his face, Thurso and Peebles would head for the distant tide-hardened edge of the *playa* like men with a mission. If they were used to his little foibles, he, Reno, knew theirs as well by now, and this was one the two of them shared, never to be outdone, especially not by fifty yards of dirty, warm grit that lodged in the hair and the recesses of the ears, grit which even found its way, in some mysterious fashion, into the very suitcases back in their hotel rooms. They had a conversation about it later as they lay on their beach beds watching the old man as he carefully raked his own little strip of territory.

Peebles said, 'You'd think it was gold-dust the way Paco looks after it.' Then, up on his elbow, '*Eh, Paco?*'

The old man, who had no English, raised his head, grinned at them then went back to his labour of love.

'Maybe there's a Tidy Beach competition,' suggested Thurso.

'First prize, a week in Blackpool,' said Reno.

'Second prize, *two* weeks!' In unison. They all laughed then, even though the joke was an old one.

Under their thatched umbrella they lay stretched like human spokes, for it was important that they didn't go back home with an obvious suntan; in Reno's case that meant none at all. Peebles, who had a new moustache and the vanity of youth that went with it, felt it was unfair that they had to retain their pallor as well; after all, Reno would be the one in the public eye not them, but Thurso was firm.

'You heard what the man back home said. None of us are here for the good of our health.'

But to all outward appearances they were, and that was the way it had to be, for all their sakes.

Reno scooped a shallow hole between his outstretched legs, inviting them to peer in.

'They brought the sand in from over there,' he said, pointing in the direction of what they took to be Africa. 'Boat-loads of the stuff.'

Thurso allowed the foreign grains to trickle slowly through his countryman's fingers, dreaming of Sahara dunes.

Peebles said, 'Where did you get that from? Out of some book, I suppose.'

'No, somebody in a bar. As a matter of fact.'

Thurso clenched his fist suddenly.

With exaggerated care, Reno blew away some grains at the bottom of the shallow pit. Tiny flecks of mica in the texture of the rock caught the light. He had lied, of course, just to see their reaction. Peebles was right, everything he knew about this island had come from a book. When you're locked up for six years as he had been, the expression 'armchair traveller' takes on an ironic meaning all its own. But that was behind him now, and, he reflected, these two were just as anxious to make him believe that as he was. To make amends he suggested they take out one of the pedalos that lay beached above the shoreline. Thurso kept his eyes closed, but Peebles stirred.

'Go with him,' said Thurso in lazy tones. 'Keep the child happy,' and they were a jolly threesome once again, putting the factory back home far behind them for ten sun-filled days. That was the story, if anyone ever asked.

Gnarled old Paco walked with them to the nearest pedalo and, taking their pesetas, watched the awkward launch of

97

one of his tiny flotilla without expression. Reno climbed on board first, placing bare feet on the treads, settling his straw hat lower on his brow, for he had read somewhere that water intensifies the sun's rays. His teeshirt, bought locally, was one of the faded millions left over from last year's World Cup while Peebles wore a singlet in nautical blue to show off his physique. Taking hold of the steering rope, he thrust down suddenly with powerful, freckled legs. Their craft spun in a circle of spume, Reno cursing as he tried desperately to match the other's vigour. Peebles laughed, eased off; then they began to move out into deeper water.

After the initial clumsiness Reno found it easy to play his part in keeping their barque on an even course. His spirits rose as the hot sun prickled his bare arms. On the far side of the bay other pedalos were setting out on their own individual voyages of discovery. Some hugged the shore, others headed boldly for the open sea. Reno suspected he would have little say in the matter when Peebles decided he belonged to the second category. But just now they were like any honeymoon couple sedately traversing the briny. The sound of the paddles was comforting, a gentle clopping rhythm, and between the twin torpedoes a calm area of water kept pace with them. Tiny shoals of fish came and went in the enclosure, glittering like scraps of silver paper. Reno concentrated on the display and, when he raised his head, felt blinded and dizzy. Peebles had ceased paddling; he was watching a water-skier sliding across the bay, a well-developed girl in a red wet-suit. There were three young people in the towing boat with their heads back laughing. They looked tanned and aristocratic in a Spanish way, and their boat followed its inexorable course as though swimmers and people like themselves were invisible.

The girl was now swimming in ever-increasing sweeps, the occupants of the speedboat shouting encouragement to her above the high roar of the motor. Reno felt fear, sensing suddenly the foreignness of these people, their unpredictability. Glancing at Peebles for reassurance he found none, for the other's face had darkened. The boat had gone past and the girl on the end of her long, long rope seemed to hurtle straight towards them. Her wet black hair streamed out behind her, and they could see her strong breasts and belly outlined by the latex of her expensive suit.

Peebles shouted, 'Jesus Christ!' as she missed them by a matter of yards and they could see the look on her face, a look of contempt. Seconds later the wash hit them and the pedalo rose and dipped alarmingly. Reno thought for the first time of all that depth of water beneath the bare soles of his feet. Clinging to the rusty iron of his chair, he heard Peebles shouting after the disappearing boat and that perfect gleaming torso.

'Fucking foreign *cow*!' he yelled. '*Bitch!*' and Reno had a sudden intimation of what must be going on in that blond cropped head; a realisation that never in a lifetime would there ever be the remotest chance of shafting someone as classy as that. Then Peebles thrust savagely down, the water foamed in their wake, and they were pulling around and back to the shore.

Thurso made no comment when they dropped down beside him in the shade, perhaps recognising the humour his young colleague was in only too well. The sun was at its zenith now. Behind them on the terrace of the hotel the tables with the umbrellas were all taken, the smell of grilling meat drifting from the kitchens. There was the beginnings of torpor in the air; even the English rowdies with their tattoos and silly hats seemed not to be roaring quite so loudly as before. They had staked out a section of the beach for themselves close to one of the hamburger and beer stands, and there they sprawled in a tangle of red and white limbs for all the world like something at Blackpool or Skegness. Reno had never been to any of those places, admittedly, but he had seen the bank-holiday newsreels like everyone else. Their own territory had been chosen for its inaccessibility. It was also something of a sun-trap and there was always a party of Swedes in residence, old people, mainly, sitting in a row with their faces held patiently up to receive the ultraviolet rays. Some of the women were topless but, as they had discovered on their first day, there was nothing arousing in all that uniformity, no matter what the nationality.

In Reno's old locker Miss Mauritius had held pride of place, and when they'd come for him there wasn't time to peel her from the khaki metal. He thought of her now, with eyes closed, lying on his stomach. She had an appendectomy scar and was running to fat – it was one of the cheaper magazines – but she never failed him after lights out when all was quiet except for the sound of the plumbing and the other sleepers deep in their own dreams of flesh. He could see her now, right at this instant, in full living colour behind his closed lids as though on a screen. Would she still be there, he wondered, or was his successor another of those zealots who only tolerated pin-ups of Connolly or Tone?

Then he opened his eyes and she disappeared. In her place was another vision only, this time, she was Nordic, youthful, perfectly proportioned and breathing. A new addition to the row of sun worshippers by the low sea-wall, she was somebody's daughter, or somebody's young wife. Twenty feet from where he lay, her legs spread as though to take the thrust of the sun, her belly gleaming with oil, she was oblivious to the effect she was having in that heartless way only the young and very beautiful can manage. Then she sat up suddenly as though sensing his foreigner's lust and, pushing back her tennis player's headband, she clasped both hands on her nape and Reno caught a glimpse of the silvery tufts in her armpits, delicate as baby hair. He dropped his head into the sand groaning in despair.

Thurso asked, 'Who's for a cold beer, then?' and set off for the bar on the terrace, a heavy man in maroon nylon shorts that his wife had bought for him and which he hadn't seen until he opened his suitcase in the hotel room. Reno and Peebles exchanged glances and grinned. Their own beach-wear was presentable, as far as they were concerned, snappy even. Reno had a sudden urge to share the blonde with Peebles, but then thought better of it. Peebles would be sure to be disgusted, liking his women shaved, in keeping

100

with his athletic preferences. As for Thurso, well, Thurso was the sort of man who had probably never even seen his own wife without all her clothes. He put the thought out of his head, closed his eyes, and let the sun and the sand work their way with his Northern city-dweller's flesh.

'You shouldn't have gone out on that thing.' Thurso had returned with the beaded bottles of San Miguel and was looking down at them, withholding the beer as though they were a couple of naughty children. 'Look at you, red as two beetroots.'

'Who the fuck cares?' snarled Peebles. 'They can't shoot you for it.'

'Speak for yourself,' quipped Reno, but the time for jokes was over.

The rest of the day was marred, for all suddenly saw how ridiculous they were sweltering on this patch of unnaturally grey sand that an old man spent his life teasing and rearranging like some sort of grubby, threadbare carpet. They might just as well have stayed in the hotel room playing cards with the shutters drawn. Despair entered Reno's soul of a kind that was new to him. He was no stranger to the emotion but this, somehow, was much worse than the variant he had grown used to back home on those long wet afternoons with unlimited time to kill. Then he had prayed for sunlight, a patch of blue through the wire-mesh, a rise in temperature to dispel the chill of concrete and grey sweating metal. Here he was overwhelmed by brightness and heat, and beauty too, he had to admit; for, at the right hour and in the right light, the bay and its crescent of hotels had a quality only glimpsed before in imagination.

One of the old Swedes detached himself from his companions and started doing press-ups on a spread rug. He was the colour of teak and the sight of that ancient twig rising and falling only seemed to deepen Reno's depression. But the afternoon passed as all the others had done and at last they slowly started to climb back to the hotel. None of them could face the beach at this hour when the air was full of frisbees, and footballers with beer bellies were haring about in a final spasm of bravado. Instead they climbed the seventy-eight hewn steps leading to the road at the top of the cliff. Peebles was able to go up at a decent trot; Thurso ran him a reasonable second; Reno took the ascent in his own sweet time as always. Half-way up he stopped to look down at the sea below. He could see patches of deep green where the weed lay anchored. A white liner slid in silence across the mouth of the bay oblivious of the roar from the beaches. It was just like a film and he had no part in it. He belonged in small damp rooms where coal fires never went out, where people seemed not to notice the lack of light outdoors as well as in, where they conspired endlessly in those same damp dark rooms. He had had his fill of conspiring and all that went with it. But, there, waiting at the top of these sunlit steps were the two men who would bring him back to all of that, and so as he climbed to join them all the jokes he used to have in such abundance seemed to have deserted him.

The road at the top of the steps, with its large dead houses set back in dusty gardens, stayed quiet for the first fifty yards, then the tempo quickened and, for the rest of the way, all was strident with the sound of recorded music, Michael Jackson's voice rising in a screech from every dark shopping cave they passed. Amidst the thickets of hanging leather belts there would be someone standing with folded arms. They shuffled past all those closed, Balearic faces, feeling the resentment directed at them; even Thurso remarked on it. Peebles revelled in the native surliness whenever he encountered it and, watching him, Reno realised it was the only approach that made sense. He and his like had made these people's island one vast garbage dump, but they had gone along with it. He thought of that niggardly coating of imported sand and, when Peebles started an argument about a label that lied on a bottle of Bacardi in one of the places, he realised just how easy it could be to run amok with all those other English-speaking hooligans through the streets. Every night since they had been here they had lain listening to them in the small hours, unable to sleep for the heat. It brought back bad memories, that familiar blend of running feet, curses, breaking glass.

When they reached their hotel Thurso looked at the bottle in Peebles' hand. 'You're stocking up a bit early with the duty-frees, aren't you?'

'No, this is for now. A celebration.'

They looked at him. He was grinning but, as always, it failed to convince. 'It's my birthday.'

'No kidding?'

Reno felt a stronger reaction was expected of him but the thought had just struck him how little he knew about these two, while they knew everything about him, including the day, year, perhaps the very hour, on which he was born. They had told him his file was this thick, holding up a thumb and forefinger more than an inch apart. The gesture had come to have a special appeal for Peebles. Reno would look up from his drink in a bar to see him grin across at him, hand raised, as though suggesting a refill, but he wasn't, he was reminding Reno of his place.

They went upstairs to Reno's room on the twelfth floor. The others took it in turns to share with him, three nights on, three off. Just now Peebles slept in the bed nearest to the window, which was obvious at a glance because he was neat to the point of obsession. Thurso's feet smelt, so it was a choice of two evils as far as Reno was concerned. From the open window came the sound of splashing from the pool below and children's voices. An English family from somewhere up North had taken possession on the first day they had arrived and, for a week, they hadn't moved from the terrace as though paralysed by the memory of all those American television portrayals of the good life. The father wore a cloth cap constantly, even at mealtimes, and remained as pale as the day he first stepped off the plane.

'How's Andy Capp looking today then?' asked Peebles. He was stretched on Reno's bed with a full glass of white rum in his hand.

Reno walked out on to the balcony and looked down at the kidney-shaped blob of blue far below.

'Not a well man, I'd say, even from this height. Watney's

Red Barrel doesn't travel well, somebody should have told him that.'

'Is he wearing the headgear?'

'No, that's what I meant.'

Peebles was at his elbow in a moment. They looked down together and began to laugh. From the bedroom Thurso shouted, 'He'll hear you, for Christ's sake!' but it only made them worse and they reeled back into the room, collapsing on to the beds.

'What's so bloody funny then?' but Thurso's fellow-feeling with another family man who was being mocked soon crumbled, or perhaps it was relief that Peebles seemed to be genuinely enjoying himself. Soon they had him laughing as well and, as the level in the bottle fell, all three donned knotted handkerchiefs like the butt of their humour oblivious far below. Another bottle was sent for, coke and ice.

'Fuck the expense. After all,' grinned Peebles, 'we're on our holidays, aren't we?'

The young waiter entered into the mood, the first time any of them had seen him smile since they had arrived, delivering the drinks with a four-star flourish, accepting his lavish tip in similar fashion, permitting himself a single familiarity before leaving. 'Scottish?'

They looked at one another. 'No. Irish.'

'Ah,' he grinned. 'We like the Irish in Spain. Much spirit. *Adiós, señores.*'

When the door closed no one said anything. It was a rare moment, all sharing the same rush of sentiment. Everyone seemed to be their friend and ally, even the comic postcard figure with his noisy brood twelve floors down. Someone had to break the mood, of course, and it turned out to be Thurso, old Thurso, who, in his slow Antrim drawl, said, 'Much spirit, eh?' They both looked at him, then at the two bottles on the bedside table, and the howls of laughter started afresh.

It carried them through the time it took to shower, shave, dress for dinner, and into the lift for the descent to the

104

marbled foyer, where the other guests roamed about ill at ease in their evening finery. More drinks followed at the bar until the doors to the dining room were unlocked by the head waiter, who had something of the gaoler in his manner and appearance. At table they joked about him and his old-fashioned jacket and striped trousers which suggested better days and a better hotel. A pervading air of dissatisfaction, it seemed to them, was the distinguishing mark of everyone born on this island. Reno tried to explain that this was the natural consequence of Franco's regime or, rather, the relaxation that followed it, but no one was in the mood for such seriousness. While Peebles and Reno kept the banter flowing, Thurso sat smiling, disposing of prodigious accounts of food and, as the courses came and went, his face seemed to burn with greater intensity. The biggest joke of all was that it was he who had caught the sun, not them. When he came to see himself in a proper mirror and proper light, for the whole hotel was as shadowy as a tomb in true Spanish fashion, that would certainly be a moment not to be missed.

He rose to replenish his plate at the buffet and they watched as he veered between the tables, a shade unsteadily, Reno noted. As he passed three women who sat together he paused, for the redhead seemed to say something to him. A moment later they shared shock when he dropped into the vacant chair, raising a glass of wine for their benefit.

Reno said, 'I don't like the one you're getting,' but the joke was wasted on Peebles he could tell.

When Thurso returned he looked sheepish. 'They're all three from Dublin,' he said. 'Married. Nice girls, the lot of them.'

'Girls?' sneered Peebles.

Thurso looked at him. 'One of them's your age.'

Reno got to his feet announcing he was badly in need of a leak and, after an exchange of glances across the table, the other two put down their napkins and rose to follow. As he stood beside Peebles in the urinal Reno reflected sadly that it would have made a pleasant change to chat up a strange woman, compliant after a day in the hot sun with the old vino beginning to do its work.

'You know something, Peebles,' he said. 'I'm tired of always seeing your dick alongside mine. No offence meant, mind.'

Peebles gave a bark of laughter. At the mirror, as he was studying his appearance, he caught Reno's glance. 'You and me, we must have a *proper* talk some time. Just the two of us,' and they moved out to join Thurso.

'Where the fuck is he?' for he wasn't in one of the deep leather armchairs where they had left him and he certainly wasn't at the bar.

'Upstairs?' suggested Reno.

'What for?'

'Sunstroke?'

They laughed but Reno knew that Peebles was worried and that he was the object of that anxiety, not the older man.

'Come and have a drink,' he said. 'I promise I won't make a run for it.'

For a moment he thought he had gone too far, for there was an unspoken agreement between the three of them never to say things like that.

Peebles looked at him. Then he grinned. 'I believe you.'

'Good,' said Reno and, at that moment, they heard Thurso's deep laugh from the terrace. The sliding glass doors were partly open and they went across and looked out. He was sitting at the edge of the darkening pool with his back to them, the three women from the dining room making a pleasing picture, arranged, as they were, around him, avid, it would appear, for whatever confidence might fall next from that big idiot's lips. Reno and Peebles looked at one another both thinking the same thing. Peebles made to move out through the doors but Reno laid a restraining hand on his arm.

'Get somebody to call him. A message at the desk.'

Peebles said, 'Good thinking,' and their hovering young waiter was pressed into service.

Sitting in the yellow armchairs they waited and watched until Thurso came hurrying in. He looked haunted, his eyes darting to the desk which was unattended at this hour but, before he could bang on the bell – his intention was plain – they called out to him.

'Lily must have rung,' he cried the moment he came across. 'Something's wrong, I just know it.'

Peebles said, 'You didn't give her a number, did you? Sid, for fuck's sake, you know we're not supposed to.'

'It's all right for you, you're not a family man.'

Reno said, 'No one called you. It was us,' to put an end to the big man's suffering.

'You pair of bastards.'

They sat looking up into the bright red face, both feeling trapped by the leather upholstery.

'Go to hell, the pair of you! And I'm sleeping on my own tonight!'

They watched him disappear into the lift and his subsequent upward progress, marked by the winking numerals over the top of the padded doors. Without thinking, Reno said, 'Leather. There's too much fucking cowhide in this place. Stinks of it.' After a pause he asked, 'Haven't *you* noticed it?'

Peebles said, 'I would say you've got a point there.'

'You would?'

'Certainly, I would.'

They sounded like a couple of drunks. Suddenly Peebles giggled. 'Did you see his face? Did you?'

'I did.'

'Like a well-skelped arse.'

They rose to their feet and, still laughing, pushed out through the hotel doors and into the blue scented night. For a moment they swayed on the marble steps. The sound of cicadas filled the air and, in that instant, they felt pierced, as never before, by the thought of just how far away from home they really were. Far above their heads were stars embedded in velvet that would never shine down on their own Northern shores. At least, that's the way they felt it

107

must be and, setting off across the dusty no-man's land in front of the hotel, they silently pondered this awesome truth.

Diagonally across from them was an English pub called the Big Lion. They hadn't got the name quite right, the owners, but the whole resort was full of misspellings to delight Reno's eye. It reminded him of home, but at least they had an excuse here. There was another sign picked out in cursive blue neon, but that certainly held no trace of ambiguity. *Happy Hour*, it read, and the words seemed to proffer just what they were in need of. They followed its lure and pushed into the dim interior. The place was empty except for a couple of waiters playing pool and three elderly tourists resting their feet and waiting for something to happen so that they could talk about it at dinner. Peebles wanted to leave instantly not wishing to squander his attractiveness even at this early hour, for there was another place further on, he said, with a ratio of three women tourists to every man. But Reno led him to the bar and placed the first order of the evening. The idea was that all drinks between eight and nine were half-price and every bar in town employed a similar decoy, but this being tourist Spain where the stuff flowed like tap-water you got two for the price of one, not quite the same thing. The practice created drunkenness on a scale and speed that had surprised even the three of them who thought they had seen more of it than most. There was one bar where they filled the arrayed tankards from a hose-pipe and the waiters wore firemen's helmets.

Half-way through the second round – they were drinking branded Smirnoff – Peebles put an arm about Reno's shoulders and, squeezing, said, 'We're better off without him. You and me – we have more in common.'

Reno kept silent while the jukebox played Donna Summers quietly in the background hoping the sentimentality he detected would disperse. The emotion was one that always made him feel uneasy, experience teaching him that it frequently was the prelude to unpleasantness, particularly in the case of someone like the man next to him.

'Where was that place you were talking about, the pick-up joint?' he asked, hoping there was not too much haste in his voice.

'Time enough for that.'

Peebles slid off his stool and led the way over to a corner table. He raised his tall glass. 'You and me have more in common than you think. It may not look like it, you in your position, the way things are, but it's true, it is true.'

Reno concentrated hard on the wedge of lime floating in his drink. Peebles clasped his knee. 'That file of yours doesn't tell the half of it. Now why don't you admit it?'

Marvelling at his own courage, Reno forced a laugh.

'Busman's holiday, is it? You might have picked a better spot for the third degree.'

Peebles looked at him with hurt in his eyes.

'Did anyone ever give you a kicking? Shocks? The hood?'

Christ, thought Reno, this is worse than I thought. 'Well, did they? Did they?'

'No, they didn't.'

There was silence except for the click of the numbered balls on the pool table. One of the tourists was studying the lighted front of the jukebox as if it was a menu.

'They 'aven't got James Last! Nowt but darkie stuff!' he called out suddenly to his party. Reno looked at Peebles. A catch-phrase like that could provide enough hilarity to last them for days. *Please*, prayed Reno, *please*.

He felt the hand leave his knee. Peebles sighed. 'I know you think we're a bit of a joke. Whoever teamed us up certainly did.'

Reno looked blank, then it dawned on him. 'You mean your names?'

'Don't tell me it never struck you before, you with all those fucking A-levels.'

It had, of course. When fear got the better of him, fear of the future, and that meant the next minute and a half, he would console himself with a grotesque image of his keepers in kilts, a double-act doing Harry Lauder numbers. 'Hoots, mon,' he said, not caring any longer.

Peebles sat staring at him.

'A braw, bricht, moonlicht night. Go on, try it. *Try it.*' And that was how he managed to put off the evil hour.

They left soon after, feeling fit to face anything, across the waste-ground, arm in arm, and singing gently. A moon had risen, their shadows moved in stately fashion before them and Reno no longer had any fear of the sudden nip at his heels that would lead to that slow and lingering death he had such bad dreams about. Instead he wondered if this open space would still be as it was if he ever returned. He thought not. During the day the sounds of building work never faltered so why should this be spared? It was strange to think, and stranger to explain, why a sun-baked acre of wasteland with scrub around the edges should be the only thing to look back on. But then he had always been drawn to the like ever since he was a child, and later there had been a neglected triangle of bracken he had lain in for three days and nights deep in South Armagh, just before he had given himself up.

They crossed the road where the bus-stop was and began the short trudge down the alleyway between the hotels. Reno began to laugh. 'Hey up, old sport, this is the way to the beach. We don't want to go to the beach,' but Peebles kept on going and he allowed himself to be hauled along over the sand. It slowed the legs, made the heart pump; more than anything he felt like throwing himself down on its soft, shifting carpet. He would stretch on his back, they would lie together side by side and let this great foreign firmament cup them in its embrace. A long-wave radio somewhere was playing tinny North African music. He wanted to stop and listen. His senses had never been so alive. Suddenly his feet were wet, a warm spreading tingle, and he struggled to free himself. 'Christ, Peebles, we're in the water!'

The eyes stared back at him, the mouth hard. 'It's not far now.'

'Where are we going, for Christ's sake? Where?'

'There,' pointing to their own part of the beach, at the foot of those seventy-eight stone steps.

Reno groaned. 'Did you leave something behind?' he said, for he could understand a stubborn obsession of that kind. 'Watch? Your lighter?'

'You know I don't smoke.'

There didn't seem to be any more point in resisting so he allowed himself to be led, like the charge he was, all his needs taken care of. He never thought of his own side of the contract if he could help it. That was in the future, in another place, far from all of this. Then they were in among the pedalos, a pale orderly shoal of them gleaming in the moonlight, and Peebles was fumbling with the rope that tethered them to a stake in the sand. Reno sat down to watch. In a moment he knew he would have to do something decisive but he wanted to put it off as long as he could.

'Now, this is silly,' he said. 'You know we don't want trouble.'

Peebles was cursing the knots. He didn't seem to hear. 'Silly,' repeated Reno and got to his feet. 'Theft, Peebles. Theft.'

The other stopped what he was doing, pierced by the word, as Reno knew he would be. His eyes grew smaller. 'We'll see Paco, old Paco, then. *Dinero.*' He held out his wallet, shaking it like an insult.

'Fuck you then, Peebles, see if I care,' but he went with him, nevertheless, to where a dim light burned in the old man's shack. Peebles knocked on the unpainted wood and a voice called out nervously from within, '*Que?*'

Peebles said, '*Amigos*,' and stood back.

The door opened a foot or so and a small boy was looking up at them. '*Padre*,' he called over his shoulder, but Peebles had pushed past and inside. He, Reno, followed. The two of them stood there in their tourist get-up and stared about them unable to adjust to the scene. At a table sat the old man surrounded by his brood, five or six, at least. A family like that seemed a marvel of potency, but without his straw hat he certainly did seem much younger, bald, too, which was a greater shock. There was food on the table in a big black

111

skillet and Reno recognised the saffron of *paella*. They could see another room at the rear and it came to them suddenly that the rest of the dwelling must run back into the solid rock. The idea that these people lived in a cave somehow made their unwanted presence much worse. Peebles felt it too and he reacted in the way his training had taught him. 'Paco,' he called out like an old friend and Reno couldn't help noticing how the children seemed to shrink back at the sight and sound of this red-faced foreigner advancing upon them. Their father showed his teeth nervously and half rose.

'Paco. Pedalo. Me want pedalo. Now. Tonight.'

Reno watched the ensuing performance with as much neutrality as he could muster. It was as if he were in the grip once more of another of those nightmares that used to plague him so painfully. He also visualised Thurso back in his hotel room dead drunk and he thought, *My God, it's me who has to be the responsible one in all of this. Me.* There was money on the table by now. The children looked on aghast as each note was carefully flattened out before their eyes. Their father however seemed to be blind to the sight of so many portraits of national heroes, his whole body moving painfully in his attempts to keep saying no, no, no, yet without seeming to give offence to the mad *inglés*. But then Peebles took something else from his wallet and held it out for the old man's inspection. Reno couldn't make out what it was at first but then he heard Peebles say, '*Policía,*' and he knew. He knew that photograph in plastic with its power to threaten in any language, even that of a poor and ignorant cave-dweller.

When they stepped out into the night they left him sitting there staring at his wall in defeat, the meal before him on the table lying cold and untasted. They walked back to the pedalos and, quickly and effortlessly, one was dragged free and down to the brink. Without a word they pushed off. When there was about a fathom of dark water beneath them, Reno said, 'That was a shitty thing you did back there.' Peebles merely grunted. 'Don't you ever see yourself as others see you, Peebles? For what you are? Or is that too painful?'

Peebles stopped pedalling. Reno did so too and in the sudden silence, broken only by the lapping water, the enormity of his words seemed to deepen.

Peebles said, 'Your name's just as funny as ours is, you know.'

'It's a nickname.'

'Doesn't matter. It's just the same. *You're* just the same.'

They sat there thinking their thoughts like a married couple about to have a row and not knowing how far each would or could push the other. 'Anyway, what gives *you* the right? Someone like *you*.'

Their craft was the only thing on the water at this hour, they had the whole bay to themselves. It should have been a matter of some personal pleasure to them but it wasn't; instead that dirty old existence of theirs had claimed them yet again. The thoughts started to boil up in Reno's brain like those shoals of tiny fish he had studied earlier. He was hearing again the soft reasonable tones of the man rehearsing him in the Portakabin, the 'script' on the table between them. It grew daily as more and more names were named, dates, details of time, place, execution. And all of that flowing from him, inexhaustibly, it seemed.

'Call me Robin,' said the man, his monogrammed cigarette-case lying open between them. 'We're all very pleased with you. You know that, don't you?'

When they came to say goodbye they shook hands and his signet ring, with its blood red stone, felt chill to the touch. He boxed the foolscap, put it in his briefcase.

'One last thing, Terry. A little holiday might be in order. We think you've earned it.'

On the night of the fourth of August I went to a man's house in Clonard and took possession of certain explosive substances and a number of detonators. The man's name was... the man's name was... Oh, God, he thought, I'm a dead man, a dead man. *The man's name was...*

Peebles was saying, 'I've done things too, you know. I'm

not proud of them, but there's no time to think straight when it's happening to you. I know you know that, and that's why we're the same. I mean, come clean, you *have* pulled the trigger, haven't you? You can tell me, I'm not that English bastard in his pinstriped suit. I know what it's like, for Christ's sake. I've done it myself. Three years ago. Out in the country. Late at night. We stopped this car and I knew the bastard was up to his neck in it. There was no way he was just about his business. The car was clean, okay, but when he opened the glove compartment how the fuck was I to know what he was...'

Reno was staring out to sea. Was that dark line really the edge of another continent? It seemed so close. If he slid into these warm dark waters and let the currents carry him... He might have no choice. If his memory had really gone on him, he was as useless to these people as a burned out light bulb.

No better than a dead man. He closed his eyes on that blue, black line of distant shore and tried again. *The man's name was... the man's name was...*

Green Roads

The old man was sitting on the bus seat buried in the bank outside his cottage when the army landrover went past in the late afternoon. It churned up the steep slope in the direction of the bog where no wheeled traffic had ever been known to go before and, as it topped the incline, the old man saw a soldier with a black face staring out at him over the tail-board. The colour was natural, not camouflage, he could tell, even though it was his very first negro. This darkie soldier held a rifle and looked straight through him as if he didn't exist. The old man sat pondering in the dying sunlight. Something, he didn't know what, held him back from going inside to tell his daughter what he had seen, yet seldom did anything like this ever happen to him. One day followed another in the same dreamlike fashion, day after day after day spent here on this old summer-seat. He stroked its warm, worn upholstery. His daughter kept saying his memory was going but it was more a case of not being able to make it do his bidding, for something remembered, but deeply submerged, about men in uniform passing this way once before refused stubbornly to surface. He would just have to wait until the memory, whatever it was, floated up of its own accord. It was just that you could never tell when; perhaps today, perhaps tomorrow, perhaps never.

The old man looked at a distant staining of smoke in the evening sky. Someone had started to burn whins on their land. The others would follow suit now, he told himself; there always had to be one to start the first fire somewhere or other, for the rest to follow.

The driver of the landrover was a corporal named Jessop

from Devizes in Wiltshire, unmarried, in his early thirties, with the reputation for keeping himself to himself. A self-contained character, some would even say dour, but then that may have been because of his background. Everyone else in the platoon seemed to be from an industrial Northern city and took much pleasure in reminding him of that fact. Even Carlton, despite the colour of his skin, would chance his luck now and again, slyly joining in. Coming from Streatham put him on an equal footing with the others, as far as he was concerned.

At the corporal's side rode the young lieutenant who had the map spread on his knees. The landrover bucked and bounced and Carlton in the rear swore fluently but the corporal stared straight ahead. A perverse pleasure was making him aim for every bump and pothole in their path for he knew that they were lost and this track they were on led nowhere. The young lieutenant, however, would not admit to the fact. It was part of his class 'thing': something the other two recognised.

On either side stretched desolate moorland the colour of the vehicle they travelled in, without break or respite for the eye. They passed sheep with splashes of dye on their fleece but they kept their heads resolutely lowered. Carlton aimed his rifle taking silent pot-shots but even he seemed to feel their chill disregard. Light rain began to fall and the rhythm of the windscreen wipers beat time with their thoughts, or it may have been the other way round, while a mood of gloom settled on the landrover and its three occupants. It was as if it had shrunk or been reduced in some way to the size of an insect crawling along under a vast and darkening sky.

There came a stretch when all heard the sump drag itself over the long, stony ridge that now seemed to bisect the track. Jessop put his foot hard on the brake and sat looking out at the gathering dusk until the lieutenant said, 'Yes, let's stop here. Get our bearings, shall we?' He marched to the front and spread his map on the bonnet and began to pore over the brown and green contours.

Carlton sang softly, 'I was onlee twentee four hours from

116

Tulsa,' until Jessop told him to be quiet. Then the lieutenant was waving him over and together they studied the map.

'You can see we're roughly here,' said the lieutenant, his finger on a line of dots hugging the contours.

Jessop noted that there were quite a number of these fine lines curving and snaking across the terrain. 'Sheep paths, sir?'

'Definitely not. No question. Perfectly passable routes each and every one of them. If we stay with this one we're on, as you can see, we'll strike this secondary road here and then it's only a matter of time before we're on course for base. The map is perfectly clear about that.'

'When was it made, sir? The map, I mean.'

The lieutenant looked at him. 'No one has more up-to-date information than we have, corporal, always remember that.'

They climbed back into the landrover and Carlton said, 'How far now?' but no one answered him. They drove on and for a time the track seemed to be improving. The lieutenant handed cigarettes around, even joked a little, and Carlton sang the whole of his song now without any trace of irony.

Then they began to descend, slowly at first but finally in a rush, scattering countless small stones loosened by the rain. These rattled off the metal beneath their feet with a noise like gunfire and the corporal went even faster as though fleeing from an invisible attacker. That was how the young lieutenant saw it. An imaginative side to his nature still lingered even after all his training. But the reality was that Jessop had spotted a steep incline ahead, one in ten at least to his eyes, despite the visibility, and he wanted to tackle it at speed. But, as it turned out, it was to be the dip at the base of both hills that was to prove their undoing. With engine roaring the landrover bounded downhill and raced across the flat stretch of track. At first their route seemed smooth, almost finished in fact, but then the corporal noticed that the wheels were slowing as though some exterior force was at work. He pressed the accelerator but the engine only

117

screamed on a higher, more maddened note. At a point half-way along this valley floor the landrover finally came to a halt, its rear wheels spinning in troughs of mud.

The lieutenant sat stiff and silent while Carlton in the back swore and gave advice. Jessop, who was an experienced driver and proud of his skills, went through every combination of gears before finally switching off the engine.

The lieutenant said, 'Is there a problem, corporal?' Carlton laughed. 'We do have four-wheel drive, don't we?'

'Correct, sir.'

'So, why do we have a problem?'

Jessop sighed and got out. Kneeling down he stared blankly at a wheel, noting with no real interest that it was already buried to the hub and appeared to be sinking. His own boots were, as well, a strange sensation and, straightening up, he walked off a few paces leaving behind well-defined tracks. The ground had a curious consistency, not quite solid. The corporal lifted a large flat rock and pitched it several yards then watched it settle in the hollow it had formed.

Standing there he was barely conscious of the fine rain on his face, or anything else for that matter. The landrover and its occupants and their plight meant nothing to him. He might have been one of those sheep they had passed earlier. He didn't feel angry, as might be expected. Instead, as he listened to the silence he felt inert as stone.

Then the young lieutenant joined him making a great play of kicking the tyres and stooping to peer underneath. The corporal stared at the back of his head, young and vulnerable under his beret, and he felt dizzy for a moment, sweating at the sudden and unexplained violence of his thoughts.

The lieutenant straightened up. 'Have we anything we can put down, an old blanket, tarpaulin, that sort of thing?'

'Not really, sir. We can't get purchase.'

'I can see that for myself, corporal.' Carlton had joined them and both he and the lieutenant were looking expectantly at Jessop now.

The the lieutenant said, 'Get me the machete, private,' and Carlton, suddenly energetic and grinning, brought it to him in its canvas sheath. 'We'll make a start by cutting some of this gorse. If it works in snow I don't see why it shouldn't do the trick in this muck as well.'

He slid out the greased blade – it had never been used – and held it out to neither of them in particular, but Jessop turned away almost fastidiously. Then Carlton seized it and began hacking at the tough stalks.

The lieutenant watched the growing pile. He was remembering with fondness one Boxing night when his MG had got stuck not far from Dorking. While the other three had laughed and continued to drink in the car he had worked like a demon among the drifts foraging and, finally, bedding the wheels with bracken and although it had been a sudden impulse on his part it had done the trick. Much later he had found out, indirectly, that the girls in particular had been most impressed but it was his own private pleasure that meant more to him, despite having ruined a perfectly good dinner-jacket.

With the mood of that snowy night still upon him he began furiously laying armfuls of the stuff around and under all four wheels. Then he stamped and pounded with his boots until the landrover seemed to be resting on a thick, sodden, brown carpet. Carlton stood watching, as did Jessop, but when he tried to signal to the corporal his amusement at the sight of this odd war dance the other turned his face away.

The lieutenant shouted, 'Let's see if *that* will do the trick!' and Jessop went over to the landrover and climbed in. For a moment he sat there as though he had never seen a dashboard or steering wheel in his life before, then, shaking his head violently, he pressed the starter. All his old skills returned to him and with infinite patience he began coaxing the engine to its task.

For a long time he hung in the seat oblivious to everything but the sounds of the motor and the straining of the transmission then, above the roar, he heard someone shouting his name and the lieutenant was at the open door.

The corporal looked at him in surprise. His face and front were coated with mud, great gouts of it. Why was he shouting, the corporal asked himself. He was genuinely confused. The lieutenant reached in and switched off the engine, then began wiping his face with his coarse mesh scarf. He spat disgustedly. Carlton came into view, winking at Jessop. 'Your driving, corp, blimey!'

The lieutenant said, 'What a God-awful, bloody country,' then he looked at Jessop who still sat grasping the wheel. 'I really think you've done enough for one day, corporal, don't you?' and his voice had taken on the leisurely drawl of his class, something the two men had never heard before.

'Looks as if we're bogged down then, sir,' said Carlton cheerfully. 'What we need is a tow.'

The lieutenant stared about him. 'Smoke over there.' He sniffed as if he could smell it. 'Now, if they have a tractor . . .'

Jessop had got out by now and, speaking quietly as if to the ground, said, 'No tractors. Not out here, not these people.'

The other two exchanged glances. Carlton was grinning again but the lieutenant's face had set hard as stone. 'Yes, you *would* know all about that, wouldn't you, Jessop?'

Then he reached under the passenger seat, pulling out the handset of the radio. They listened to him talking to base, explaining their plight and position on the map, and at first his voice was patient and unhurried just as if he was speaking to one of them. But then there were angry blizzards of static from the other end and they could hear him protesting.

At one point he said, 'Some joker must have turned the signposts around, sir,' and it registered with Jessop even in his dulled state that he had been right about the lieutenant all along. But there was no satisfaction in the knowledge. He was standing a little way off by himself with his head raised as if he was picking up signals of his own from the air.

They were in a glen of sorts, ringed on all sides by moorland, the rim blue-black and clearly defined against the sky. The low murmur of running water could be heard nearby. Jessop felt something he could not put into words. It was as if he had stood like this in such a place once before in a dream. For a dizzy moment he seemed to be looking down on to the scene from a great height, the landrover the size of a matchbox toy, himself a figure tiny in scale a little way off. He felt, he felt – it seemed to him he was on the point of getting to the secret core of it when the moment passed and the lieutenant shouted for him to return to the landrover.

He was sitting in the front with a look on his face that said he would be doing everything strictly by the book from now on. 'No tow truck until o-nine-hundred hours, I'm afraid.'

The grin left Carlton's face. *'Tomorrow!'*

The lieutenant ignored him. 'So it looks like a night on the bare mountain for us all, chaps.' A wintry little smile at his private joke came and went.

'Jesus Christ, sir!' Carlton cried out. 'Not out *here*!' His grip had tightened on his weapon while his eyes went darting about him.

'Oh, relax, private, you're not in bandit country now. Certainly not around here. Believe me, I do know.' And he did, for it was something he took pride in, the young lieutenant, his 'demography', as he liked to call it back in the mess.

'I don't care a toss what side they're on, you can 'ave 'em! Bleedin' sheep-shaggers, the lot of them!'

The lieutenant laughed, looking at Jessop as he did so, but the corporal had returned once more to his own private world.

'Come,' said the lieutenant, jumping out of the landrover, 'we must build a shelter before it gets too dark.'

Carlton grounded his rifle in disbelief. 'Shelter! Sir?'

The lieutenant held out the machete, but this time it was clear that it was intended for Jessop. For a moment the corporal weighed it in his hand, looking at it strangely, then he began clearing a patch a little way off where the ground was firm. The corporal worked slightly bent at one knee, the blade cutting low and close, and there was such economy

121

and ease about the operation that the other two watched in silence. Heaps of the tawny gorse began to rise about the sides of a perfectly formed rectangle. The revealed sward was pale and cropped and the lieutenant stared at its perfection. An anger was growing in him for what he and the private were witnessing was nothing more, it seemed to him, than yet another ploy intended to make him look foolish.

'All right,' he managed to call out at last. 'All right, you've made your point!' but Jessop continued to work on.

The lieutenant's face became redder. Rising, he strode across to the toiler, laying a hand on his shoulder. Instantly he felt the heat of the man's body through the khaki wool and, in the same moment, Jessop jerked as though stung. Then he raised a face with such savagery in it that the lieutenant fell back. They both looked down at the blade in the corporal's hand, then the moment passed.

The lieutenant called out, 'We'll bed down here,' striking a heel deep in the turf. Then he made off in the direction of the stream, tracking it by sound, for he felt certain there would be saplings growing there, and he was right, too. But before doing a thing he carefully wiped the haft of the machete and his own hands to remove all traces of the corporal's sweat.

Carlton said, 'Answer me one question, just one question,' when the lieutenant disappeared from sight. 'Why can't we just kip in the 'rover? I mean, did we join the boy scouts, or what?' He offered Jessop a smoke from his tin but the corporal declined.

'No?' said the other, then he leaned close. 'Here, what you on, man? You're on something, ain't you, sly old sod.'

The corporal got up from the bumper and moved back to the space he had just cleared. He stood there at its heart while Carlton continued to eye him slyly.

'Give us a taste, man,' came that soft voice. ''Cause I know you're on something, that's for sure.'

Jessop turned his head away as if to hide the evidence, though the truth was that he had taken nothing, never had for that matter. Something deep-seated had always made him shy clear of such things, even now when the right pill could see him through this. For two weeks he hadn't slept. He wondered how long he would be able to keep going. A numbness and a trembling had begun in one of his legs and he knew his reactions were slowing, but he didn't want any help from anything or anyone. The word punishment entered his head for some reason. He supposed this must be his way of punishing himself, his body, for that night in the pub car-park near Swindon. He closed his eyes, breathing in deeply, willing himself to remember. The images began to burn.

It had been the last night of his leave and it had been a pub picked at random, not that he was a great one for pubs, never had been, but before going back for another tour of duty something made him walk into this place in the heart of the country. He had imagined what it might be like inside, horse-brasses, oak settles, a real fire of logs even, and it was as he'd pictured it, something to remember over there, take the edge off things when it all started getting you down. He ordered a pint and sat in a corner out of the way, a habit, when he heard this man at the bar. There were other people in the place as well, regulars, but the man's accent, although it was soft, seemed to go through him like a knife. He began to tremble, he didn't know why, sitting there with his tankard in front of him, and as the time passed and the stranger with the brogue began to talk more and more loudly he found he couldn't rise to go up for a refill. He just listened and shook with lowered eyes. Nothing like this had ever happened to him before, such a terrible hatred for a complete stranger. There seemed no answer to it. The man was neither a bully nor loudmouth; he seemed genuinely liked in the place. It was obvious, too, that he was country-bred, like everyone else there, himself included, nothing could disguise it. At one point he did cry out passionately, 'Don't call me *Pat*. I'm not a *Pat*. I'm as British as the rest of you. Nobody knows our history. *Our* history. Or cares,' and

123

they all laughed at him. Then he laughed, too, and ordered a round for the house and Jessop, in his corner, knew it was time to go for he felt he mustn't allow his hate to be diluted, so he quickly rose and walked out.

In the car-park in the dark he waited for almost an hour, it seemed, before the man came out to relieve himself. He was singing, something sad like all their songs, and even when Jessop felled him he still continued to sing a little. Then the kicking began in earnest, for the corporal had been trained to inflict the utmost damage as speedily and as effectively as possible and he had been taught well, yet the man curled up on the ground barely uttered a sound, a protest or cry, even, while it was happening to him. Almost as if he felt he deserved it in some strange way.

That was a fortnight ago and he had walked off into the night not knowing or caring if the heap on the ground was alive or dead. The following day he was back on patrol, over here, on the stranger's own terrain.

The corporal looked down now at the carefully mown patch of turf at his feet. Punishment. The word came into his head again. How long must he have to wait? Not long now, he told himself, almost soothingly, not long now, for it seemed to him, standing here in this place, that he had already prepared the ground for it.

Returning with his booty the young lieutenant saw the corporal standing there as though defending his newly-acquired territory. The sight displeased him for some reason and he shouted out for him to come and give a hand, dropping his burden where it lay. At the stream, he had carefully trimmed, then pointed the stakes and the look of them lying together now so healthy and still full of sap filled him with pride. Already he could smell the never to be forgotten tang of his old tree-hut in the garden at Weybridge.

He watched while Carlton and the corporal constructed a rough shelter using the materials at hand and when it met finally with his approval they all stood back to look at it.

124

Darkness had crept up and with it a chill mist. Carlton shivered dramatically. 'How's about a nice little fire, then, sir?'

'No fire. No lights.' The lieutenant's face seemed to have lost its youthful outline in the little light remaining.

'But you said it was all right, sir. Out here, sir. No bandits, remember, sir?'

'I know I did. Another thing, no smoking, either. I'll take the first watch.'

He waited until they crawled inside the makeshift bothy before going over to lean against the side of the grounded landrover. First watch, he knew, was the soft one to draw but he didn't care, that was his prerogative. He was piqued, as well, if the truth were known because, too late, he'd realised that he would have to share his hut, when what he really wanted all along was to have it all to himself the way he remembered it from those long magical school holidays.

Carlton and the corporal lay in the close, itchy darkness, side by side, not talking, because they both knew the lieutenant was only a matter of yards away. A low moaning sound was the nearest Carlton could get to his greatest desire which was to complain loudly and at length. He tossed and turned on their bed of bracken while the corporal lay unmoving, staring up at a gap in the low roof. Presently a star could be seen framed there. It looked like an eye to the corporal but the thought didn't disturb him. Ever since they had arrived in this place he had felt he was being watched. All he could do now was wait, he told himself, for whatever was out there to catch up with him. It was only a matter of time.

At midnight by his watch the lieutenant put his head into the darkness of the shelter. Carlton was snoring steadily, the corporal lay alongside, silent as a log, and the lieutenant smiled to himself, for the past four hours on his own had, strangely enough, smoothed away all his earlier vexation. These were his men, he thought fondly to himself, see how they depended on him. The way they slept out here in this place so trustingly was the measure of that. He decided he

125

was a lucky man after all, that he really had found his true vocation. He put out a searching hand to grasp Carlton's ankle, it really had to be done, when he felt another hand take his before it could close on the sleeper's foot. A voice from the darkness said quietly, 'I'll take the next watch, sir,' and the corporal's body slid swiftly past and out into the night air before he had time to think or make any sort of reply.

A full moon had come out by this time and Jessop felt dwarfed by the glare. He hunkered down; his shadow contracted even more. Far off somewhere the cry of an animal in pain quickly came and went and he was left to his watch.

As he crouched there, everything about him seemed to imprint itself upon his brain with terrible clarity as if he could read the landscape like no one else before or since. Grasping a tussock of grass to anchor himself he saw how the encircling rim of hills ran with barely a dip in its outline even where the track entered and left it, and the track itself had a similar perfection of line. It brought to mind old Roman routes from his own part of the country yet he had read that no Roman had ever set foot here. Before, it had lain there barely visible to the eye but now, by this trick of the light, the path had come back into its own. He thought of all those other old forgotten tracks lying hidden on the lieutenant's map and only returning to life like this while people slept.

The lethargy had left him now; his brain felt clear and responsive. He looked at the landrover, then at the shelter where the others were sleeping, oblivious. The landrover looked as though it had sunk even further, was still sinking, in fact. As for the shelter, it seemed reclaimed already; nothing but a handful of sticks and dying grasses. The corporal knew with total certainty now that he would never leave this place. It was an irony, even though it barely registered, for it to happen to him out here, he thought, in such a setting, and not in some alleyway in the city he had left that morning, the way he'd always expected it to be. And

126

so he waited almost calmly, for he knew he could take the last watch as well if it was to take that long.

But then something strange and most unusual happened. The corporal fell asleep out there in the open and when he awoke, stiff and damp, the moon had gone and in its place a ribbon of light was beginning to brighten the sky to the east. He rubbed his eyes and tried to get up from where he had fallen. Instinct made him reach out in a panic for his weapon but it was there by his side, wet to the touch. Then he looked up and, where the distant rim of the high moor was turning to pink, he saw a number of objects breaking its outline. They looked like fencing posts at first, but then he saw that they weren't spaced evenly and that they varied in height and bulk as well. He shielded his gaze with his hand, squinting into the growing light, and then at last he saw what they were. At least thirty motionless figures stood there looking down at him and even at that distance he could feel the terrible intensity of their gaze. There was great patience there as well, it seemed to him, as if, while he slept, they had waited without movement or complaint. He began to notice other things as well. Most of them held implements in their hands, a few scythes, but mainly pitchforks and long poles tipped with metal. Their clothes looked outlandish as well, old and worn out from the effect of weather and long drudgery in the open.

Jessop, the corporal from Wiltshire, stood there as though on trial but already knowing the verdict. He felt calm and curiously rested. The watchers on the horizon had made no move but by now he knew they never would. There was a great silence all around. It was time. The corporal knelt down and, taking off his beret, laid it on the ground by his side. He took up his rifle. Its metal was cold and damp to the touch from where it had lain on the grass and, as he brought the barrel up under his chin, the last thing to reach his senses was the pungent odour of gun-oil.

Propped up in bed – it was the only way he could sleep now he found – the old man came sharply out of a fitful dream.

127

He listened for the sound that had woken him to come a second time but it refused. A sharp crack like the snap of a dry twig but distant, very distant, that was all the impression he was left with. The window was brightening now: he watched the room take form. At this hour he had only his thoughts to occupy him, his daughter wouldn't stir until her alarm went off in the middle of the morning, so he allowed memories, fragments of the past, free play.

On the wall facing him was a posed photograph of his own father holding a Union Jack and a curved ornamental sword. He could barely remember him yet, strangely, everything about his grandfather would always fall into sharp focus. He had been thinking about him only last night in the kitchen and about the way he had of slowly lifting live coals out of the fire between finger and thumb to light his pipe, when it had come to him about the soldiers going up the bog road. It was a story from the old, almost forgotten days when every house had a pike buried in the thatch in readiness for the call. Then, after the big battle and the rout, a troop of Fencibles, that was the name his grandfather had called them, were supposed to have ridden past this way in pursuit of some rebels, another unusual name for people from these parts. But the English troopers had got caught in the bog, men and horses sinking, so the story went, deep in the moss, and after a time the men in brown coats, as they were known, came down from the high ground and piked all of them to death. No trace had ever been found, not a bone or a belt buckle. All that remained was an old story, for the bog never gave up any of its secrets.

The old man thought of the road; he hadn't been that way for twenty years. It used to be a beautiful, wild place even then. In time no one would even remember that a track had once run that way. It would all go back to its original state; soon he, himself, would be joining it. The old man wept a little, for no one likes to contemplate that sort of thing without some sadness.

The Hands Of Cheryl Boyd

On the afternoon in question they came over the brow of the hill, a compact little group, the two women on either side and the juvenile pushing Cheryl in the wheelchair. In his later reconstruction of events the Inspector left the impression of a grim-faced raiding party sallying out from the estate at the head of the town to descend on defenceless shopkeepers. In reality, all four were in a fit of giggles, for Julie Ann, whose house they had all started out from, would keep on referring to more and more terrible things. She had already drunk the best part of a bottle of sweet Martini that morning; and now she was on to her favourite topic, a cigarette clinging to her lip.

Outside Barr's funeral parlour they came to a halt. Maisie was blue in the face; they were still laughing, but they could see she had to find a moment or two on a bench. While the older woman caught her breath and Julie Ann held her cigarette to the juvenile's, Cheryl gazed about her with her customary calm expression. Her hands lay on the plaid rug, palms down, to show them off to their best advantage, for everyone remarked on their distinction.

Much later Harold Duff was to be drawn by their delicate pallor, long after he knew, in his heart of hearts, the terrible risk he was running each time he visited their owner. But how, he persuaded himself, could such perfection find any place in the sordid picture painted by that newspaper report? There was something Victorian about Harold, despite his youth, something yearning. Alas, never would he be able to break the habit of trying to read character in people's eyes and mouths and, of course, in Cheryl Boyd's case, her almost perfect hands.

She examined them now, turning them this way, then that. They were her dearest asset. She didn't need the others to tell her just how fine they were; she knew. They would all take it in turns to fondle them. Julie Ann would lay her own toil-worn specimens alongside on the warm wool and, if she had been tippling, she would cry a little. When her husband left her she had lost custody of the two children. Their photographs were on the sideboard, a boy and a girl in sailor-suits, Darren and Denise, the glass in the frame smudged from all the drunken kissing that went on.

Cheryl smiled to herself as the traffic hummed past. She never felt bored, not when she had her thoughts to keep her company. Over the years she had cultivated an alert look. People remarked on it before they noticed her hands.

'Next stop inside. Eh, girls?' Maisie joked, a reference to the funeral parlour.

They all laughed at that and the older woman's eyes brightened. She touched her hair, girlishly almost. 'What do you think? A wee rinse?'

They looked at her, then at Cheryl.

'You can always tell dyed hair,' she said carefully. 'No matter what,' and the others were lost in admiration, as always. They continued on their way down past the Chinese take-away, Lorraine's, the Frontier Bar, the newly opened video shop. Cheryl found it all fascinating. The others were infected as well and the conversation died as their eyes darted about them. Anyone seeing them at this particular juncture might well have been forced to agree with the prosecuting Inspector's description, but then everything is deceptive about this story. And so they proceeded at the same leisurely pace, the pale rubber wheels of the chair softly murmuring and Cheryl gazing about her at everything with as much interest as if she were on a first visit to some foreign resort.

She was wearing pastel shades, because of the time of year, and although others in the same condition might not have bothered, beneath the rug her skirt was fine pleated terylene and her tights had come out of their wrapping only

130

that morning. Such private knowledge gave her satisfaction. The smile on her face said as much, but it was a smile carefully modulated so as never to give offence.

As they were passing the Starlight Lounge, someone called Julie Ann's name and, turning, they saw a red-faced man swaying in the doorway. They checked their pace while Julie Ann went back to speak to him, all being careful not to stare, except the juvenile, who knew no better. When Julie Ann caught up with them her mouth was set tight.

'Brownlees,' she said. 'The worse for wear,' although they could see that for themselves plain enough. He had been her husband's best friend before the break-up and ever since had been pressing his attentions on Julie Ann every chance he got. Men, it seemed, had tendencies in that direction; even Maisie could corroborate that little item of information from bitter personal experience. She had no time for any of them, she declared, not since her own wedding night. Whenever she said that, all three would look meaningfully at Cheryl, as much as to say, at least you won't have to concern yourself with any of *that*.

They walked on, but now it was as though a cloud had passed across their sunny firmament. Julie Ann kept biting her lip and they could see that the encounter had brought it all back, all the old heartache. Cheryl could think of nothing whatever to say, neither could Maisie, but the juvenile, for some perverse reason of her own, launched into a long and tedious account of a fatal accident she had read about. If they had let her she would have happily gone on right to the gory end, but that would have made Julie Ann even more down in the dumps, for she had nightmares about her own two mites being run over and not being able to get to the hospital on time.

Outside Wellworth's they stopped. The day seemed ruined. What were they doing here in the middle of town like this? Why had they come? They felt out of place. There was always nervousness about starting out, for their estate had a bad name. Now that same old anxiety returned. They felt people were staring at them, at their appearance. Cheryl experienced a much deeper moment of panic. She looked down at her hands, but that smartly dressed woman with her little daughter saw only someone pathetic in a wheelchair. A moment later the same hurrying woman seemed to glare at them for taking up so much of the pavement.

On an impulse Cheryl dropped her hands to the wheels, something she would normally never do, and pushed herself at the big glass doors. They whispered apart and she found herself inside the store, facing the check-outs and the four girls in their crisp grey overalls seated at the tills. They had their backs to her but she felt that at any moment they would turn in unison to stare at her. She knew there would be hostility there, no matter what, all her power to please of no avail.

Then the doors sucked breath again and the others were alongside, Julie Ann shaking the chair handles gently. 'Little Miss Independent,' she muttered, but with no trace of rebuke in her voice, none. So much so, in fact, that it seemed to Cheryl she must hold on to that illusion of herself at all costs, it was so attractive; so, laughing gaily, she broke away, for the second time that day, propelling herself towards the aisles. For a moment they stared after her, then at each other, then set off in pursuit, Maisie, the responsible one, grabbing up a wire basket as she went.

At the toiletries Cheryl was waiting for them with her head to one side and a smile on her face, a mischievous smile with the power to melt stone. Not that they would gainsay her anything, for, quite suddenly, they felt united again, could laugh freely at everything and everyone in this one-horse town, just like before. Cheryl reached up to the shelves and took hold of a bottle of shampoo, Apple Blossom for flyaway hair. She held it out for Julie Ann's inspection, it was the brand she always favoured, then, in a single quick movement, she had slipped it out of sight and under her rug. Maisie went pale. She gestured mutely with the basket. The others burst out laughing in the instant at the expression on her poor suffering face. She began to

132

smile herself. The juvenile took up her old position behind the chair and the little raiding party began to move purposefully off down the aisles ...

It was three months later that Harold Duff read about the case in the local paper, the headline designed to shock and horrify, *Wheelchair Used in Shoplifting*. He was sitting at the card table his landlady had provided when he had mentioned that he intended to spend a good deal of his time in study. What he had hoped for, of course, was something much more solid and substantial, a roll-top with pigeon-holes was his dream, but he accepted the treacherous legs and the worn baize with humility. He was given to setting brakes on his pride, or what he saw as pride. In fact his whole life, it seemed, tended to unroll in a series of jerks. He would laugh out loud whenever this truth struck him.

Mrs Greer, in the downstairs part of the house, was troubled whenever that high mirthless bark rang out from above. She would shake her head and think depressing thoughts about her widowhood and how vulnerable she was, having a stranger in the house, but then the image of that tall young man, with the stoop and the bad skin, would put her mind at rest. She had discovered a hoard of Jacob's water biscuits in his room; nothing else in the way of nourishment, she became convinced, ever passed his lips. No wonder his complexion was the state it was. Did men have complexions? She smiled at that and went back to her mending, full of warm maternal feelings for her God-fearing young lodger.

Meanwhile, Harold sat upstairs with the newspaper spread before him. Every Thursday when it was delivered he would spend the best part of an hour studying each and every item, including the advertisements, finishing up with the deaths column. This last he regarded as the most important, from his point of view, as someone whose mission in life was to bring salvation to this town of fifteen thousand-odd souls. From an early age he had convinced himself his vocation lay among those who had lost their way

133

so, he reasoned to himself, that when bereavement struck, people would be at their most receptive to his message. Unfortunately, on each occasion so far when he had arrived at a house with drawn blinds, he had been met with suspicion and, occasionally, downright hostility. He had put this down to the fact that he had no affiliation with any of the better known churches. There was a framed scroll in his room from an obscure American bible college, but whenever he mentioned the name of the sect the faces would close against him a second before their doors did.

On Sundays, if the weather was clement, he would take up position on the steps of the town hall, bible in hand, and address the drifting populace. A few teenagers with transistors might sit grinning at him from the pedestrian precinct, but his net usually remained empty. If it was wet, he would hold a meeting in an old gospel hall near the railway tracks. The rain would drum on its rusty roof and he would offer balm to the huddled handful of old people who had come expecting something a lot more full-blooded. It was hard not to feel disappointed afterwards in his room. Kneeling on Mrs Greer's rag rug, he prayed for a breakthrough. The word always made him feel he was still at one with those robust alumni in their light-weight suits and crew-cuts, whose successes he read about in the *College Annual*. And then he opened the *Chronicle* and there, in the middle of that catalogue of weekend assaults and drunk-driving cases, he came upon the shocking headline. Something, he knew not what, made him take scissors to the paper, which was not his own. For a time the clipping lay on his table, then later he folded it so as to have it fit between the pages of his pocket testament.

Mrs Greer was taken aback when her paper was returned to her. That square gaping hole, too big for a photograph, it seemed to her, intrigued mightily, but she was not to know just how haunting the missing paragraphs were to become to her Harold over the days that were to follow. In fact, there was no real need for him to keep the cutting at all any longer. Whole sentences would rise unbidden as he went about his daily tasks. Shaving, he would mouth, 'All four defendants went into Wellworth's store and stole a bottle of shampoo, a box of Milk Tray, a packet of hairslides and a bunch of grapes, total value £3.14½. Boyd, Crawford and the juvenile then stole a £12.50 child's electric organ from House and Home. Inspector Dunseith said the organ was concealed in the back of Boyd's wheelchair. Boyd, Crawford and the juvenile also stole a pair of trousers and a jumper valued at £12.84 from Crazy Prices before being caught by a store detective from Wellworth's.'

It was the girl in the wheelchair who had worked her way into Harold's heart. The others in the case remained dim and shadowy; he felt they were probably hard-faced; that was only a supposition but, amazingly, he had the clearest picture of the one the paper kept referring to as Boyd all the time. To him, of course, she was Cheryl already.

'The defendant suffered from spina bifida and was only able to walk short distances. At the time of the crimes she was confined to a wheelchair, following an operation. Mr Trevor Arthur, who appeared for Boyd, said: "It was unfortunate that use was made of the wheelchair and this is the serious aspect of the case." He added that his client was not mentally incapacitated in any way. She knew she had acted wrongly. However, she had been influenced by the others and her aunt, with whom she lived, was deeply shocked by the incident.'

Harold stared at his soaped face in the mirror and whispered the girl's name. He was trembling. To think that the moment should come like this, and from such a source too. Already he could see the tears of redemption on those soft young cheeks. He heard his own voice soaring with divine inspiration, as they prayed together. Who could blame him if he went a little too far in fantasy, for there he was, pushing a wheelchair on to a floodlit stage, and a roar was in his ears, rhythmic chants of *hallelujah! hallelujah!* ringing out from the multitudes who had come from far and near to witness this great new Crusade and its young director.

Later he lay in his pyjamas staring up at Mrs Greer's back bedroom ceiling, waiting for the stinging in his cheeks to subside. He always shaved last thing at night, for the growth of his beard was meagre, to say the least. Tomorrow he would make his way to the girl's house and there let the good Lord breathe His power into him. He knew he would find her there, for the paper had said she was out on bail of £300, pending an appeal at the county court in two month's time.

When the doorbell rang, Cheryl was watching afternoon television with the sound turned off; a man and woman taking it in turns to grin at her from two high stools. The man held a stuffed panda in his left hand while his right did all the work. Cheryl hated their cheerfulness. She made up stories in her head about how they couldn't stand each other when the programme went off the air. The man insulted the woman; she slapped his face; he poured water over her from the jug on the table. That would have made a much better show, she thought, the mood she was in.

The bell chimed a second time but she made no move. No one could see in through the net curtains, and ever since the court case her aunt had taken to her bed. There had been quite a few malicious calls, as well, mainly from the children of the estate. She always knew they had resented her hereabouts and to have such corroboration provided a kind of grim satisfaction. Another ring, or rather three to be accurate, making up the ascending little trill. Silently, she wheeled herself to the edge of the window but nothing could be seen through the narrow space, only the dead patch of soil outside, the empty street, and the house across the way. It was a vista that just about summed up her life at the moment. Then she heard the letter-flap rattle in the hall and she sent the chair heading softly towards it. She was in time to see what looked like a circular come through and drop on the mat. She glared at it. Why couldn't they have just put it through without all the hullabaloo? Then she heard a voice. It called her name.

'Miss Boyd? Miss Cheryl Boyd? Are you at home?'

136

She felt shock now, exposed in the hallway, as though whoever was out there could pierce the solid thickness of the wood. She held her breath.

'Miss Boyd? I'm not a hawker, I assure you. A moment of your time is all I ask.'

There was silence and Cheryl felt dizzy with the lack of oxygen in her lungs.

'Very well. I shall call again tomorrow at the same time.'

At reckless speed the girl rolled back to the window but by the time she got there he had gone, walking off in the other direction, whoever he was.

It took her a long time to pull herself together. She stared at the television; the test-card had come up and the pattern seemed to quiver in sympathy, for her hands were shaking perceptibly, a vein beating in the wrist like a tiny, anxious, blue worm. It wasn't until much later that she remembered the circular in the hall, but it wasn't a free offer or any of that double-glazing rubbish either as she had supposed. She took up the leaflet and started to read the testimony of a man with a business, a wife, kiddies and a lovely home who, because of gambling and strong drink, had lost all. Then, once day, when he was as low as he could possibly get, he caught a glimpse of a child's laughing face in a school playground and, from that hour, he forsook his evil ways and found the good Lord. The story ended there, Cheryl suspected, because the paper had run out as well. She felt cheated in a dull, not terribly caring way. And no mention of sex in the man's downfall either, just whisky and horses, as if *it* didn't exist. *It*, according to Julie Ann, was everywhere, and the man wasn't born who could resist it.

Cheryl sat there, with the text in her hand, staring into space and wondering if Julie Ann was still talking about her favourite topic in that place where they had put her. She gave a little moan; she didn't care to think about any of that, and was about to throw the paper in the fire when she noticed writing on the back. Somebody had written, *You are never alone, no matter how dark the hour*, and, in spite of herself, she shivered, because the room did suddenly seem

much darker. Even with the light on, she felt no easier and
so began a restless rolling about the downstairs part of the
house. A presence had somehow invaded her life, bringing
to mind the sampler she had once seen which read, *The
Unseen Guest At The Head Of Every Table.*

Her nervousness remained with her the rest of that day
and night too, and spilled over into the following day. She
couldn't bear to have the television on, or anything else that
might distract from the moment when the doorbell would
ring. But then, when it did sound – with a thunderous peal, it
seemed, in that tomb of a house – she raced her chair into
the hallway and stopped short to stare at the back of the
door, incapable of thought or movement of any kind. The
soft patient voice repeated its refrain, the folded pink paper
fluttered down as before, the footsteps faded. She could not
believe it had turned out like this a second time. Returning
to the living room and the dead grey television, she kept
bumping into things as if she were a stranger. This time the
handwritten message read, *The good Lord seeth and
forgiveth all. Trust in Him and His infinite mercies.*

The next day she stayed in bed, bundled up under the
covers, a lump of misery, sucking her thumb. Distantly, the
bell rang as before, and if there were footsteps, she didn't
hear them. And so it went on like that until three more
reminders of her anguish lay there among the drift of
unopened letters in the hall. This man, whoever he was,
would go on like this, she could see that now. He would
never give up, no matter what. A plan, something half-
formed, began to rise inside her. She had no idea of its
outcome, but if she acted step by step she would arrive there
all right. She took a knife from the kitchen drawer, the small
wooden-handled one her aunt used to peel vegetables, and
placed it under the rug that covered her knees. Remembering that was how everything bad had started with her in
the first place, she wept a little. Then she told herself she had
been driven to it, she had, she had, and now this stranger
with his whispering through letter-boxes and his pink pieces
of paper was bringing out the criminal side of her again.

138

Everybody had a criminal side, after all; only she had found that fact of life out far too late.

'Oh, Lord,' he prayed, 'you know I'm a patient man,' but his face was hot and his hands clenched to belie the words. 'A long time I've waited for my breakthrough. Others might well have given into despair, but I haven't, Lord, you know I haven't...'

He was walking along the curving road that led down into the estate, and because of this, and the fact that his lips weren't moving, it couldn't really be said to be a proper prayer, but it was heartfelt, it most certainly was, all right. It was a Saturday and the place was almost deserted. From his patient reading of the paper he knew that all the men, and many of the women too, were in the public houses of the town drinking their Social Security money. The reported violence began in the late afternoon when that money ran out and they returned home without the shopping. He had about an hour, he calculated, to carry the day before the first police car made its appearance. The sun smouldered through a haze and his acne blazed. He was wearing a heavy suit in charcoal grey, but he only exulted in the discomfort it caused him. Several children, at a loose end, began to follow him silently, drawn by his appearance and the fixed smile on his face. He pretended not to notice them but, secretly, was rather pleased.

When he reached the house he stopped and looked about him. His fearless, moving glance seemed to take in the whole of the estate and its godless inhabitants. He smiled at the children, who drew back a little, then he marched up the short path and rang the doorbell. After each stab at the button he drew back to look up at the upper windows. They were curtained against the world, but no earthly material was a match for the Lord's penetrating power, he told himself.

The watching children, three boys and a girl, could hardly believe their eyes when the man in the dark suit and the short American haircut suddenly flung his arms aloft and began to pray, standing up in the middle of the Boyds' path. They couldn't be said to be churchgoers, in any sense, but in their short lives they had seen everything they needed to know about religious mania. Still, this was something new, and the two older boys moved closer.

'Oh, Lord,' they heard the man cry out, 'open this shuttered heart and let in the burning rays of thy salvation. Cauterise the wounds of shame and cleanse the garment of wrongdoing. Lead this young girl to thy merciful waters, and, taking her hand in thine –'

To the boys' intense disgust, just at this interesting juncture the door was flung open, they couldn't see by whom, and the man advanced up the path, crying, 'Hallelujah! Hallelujah!' to disappear inside. The disappointed little band hung around, hoping for further developments, but the door remained closed on whatever drama was taking place within. They did toy with the idea of ringing the bell but that game had lost its savour.

Instead they disappeared, viciously kicking a tin can, until the street was empty and still once more.

Upstairs in the front bedroom the girl's aunt moaned softly in her drugged sleep. Someone had been yelling in the street and the sound had broached the front line in the tranquillisers' defence. Then it seemed to her, through clouded senses, that the sound was coming not from outside, but from her own living room. With furred tongue and bleary eyes, she pulled her wrapper on and made her way unsteadily to the bedroom door, with no thought in her poor head for her own safety, none whatsoever. Not that she cared, not any more. If she hadn't been dosed silly, she told herself, she would have been drawn to every high building, every railway bridge, every accident black spot, a moth to a flame. In a mere matter of weeks she had become like one of those women on the television serials, whose lives keep taking a downward path, with never any let-up in sight.

At the foot of the stairs she held on to the bannisters, breathing heavily for a moment, then lurched into the living room. She tried to scream but her throat was too dry, for

140

there was a strange man on his knees before Cheryl's wheelchair, holding the tyres so that Cheryl couldn't move. He was sweating, his head was thrown back, and his eyes were closed, while Cheryl sat like stone, staring straight ahead of her. The aunt felt as though she had stumbled into someone else's bad dream. She was still upstairs in bed, she told herself, but she couldn't hear the tick of the baby alarm and that made her frightened. Then the man in her living room, in the dream, let go the wheels and shuffled backwards, still on his knees, raising both arms ceiling-wards as he did so. His lips moved but no sound emerged, and Cheryl's aunt had an awful feeling that she had gone deaf, as well as demented, for the television was silent, she noticed for the first time, even though a black and white western was showing. Just as Randolph Scott was ladling a glass of punch for himself at the barn dance, her niece rose slowly out of the chair, the rug falling away, and the kneeling stranger found his voice. Either that or her hearing had been restored to her for, indeed, the room rang with cries of, 'Miracle! Miracle! God's own miracle!' And at that point Cheryl's aunt tumbled to the floor in a dead faint, not because her living room had seen a divine visitation – she knew full well that the girl's legs weren't totally incapable – but because she caught the gleam of something she recognised in Cheryl's right hand.

When she came round she was on the settee and the stranger was holding a glass to her lips. His own right hand was wrapped in one of her tea-towels, she noticed, but the matter was never referred to between them again. Anyway, he had a silly smile on his face at the time, as though he was the happiest mortal on earth and, in the days that were to follow, she noticed it was also his favourite word. If he wasn't saying it, he was singing it – 'Happy, happy happy...' – but, as for Cheryl, she only seemed to become more and more morbid. All the spark seemed to have gone out of her for, despite everything that had happened, the aunt had to admit that she had always had a mind of her own, no one could gainsay her that.

The young man had by now become a regular visitor, bursting in on them at all sorts of unexpected times with face ablaze. Harold, he made them call him, and it was only a short time after this that the aunt began to notice that he himself had taken to calling her niece Cherith. The two women seemed to bend before the blast of his fervour. The hymn singing and prayers in the living room, where the television squatted now, cold and silent, passed over them like some disturbing current from foreign parts. They allowed it to steer them at will and soon Cheryl was accompanying Harold to the mission hall. The two of them became a familiar sight in the estate, the town, as well, the young man in the clerical suit and the crew-cut pushing the girl in the wheelchair. Anyone who recognised her from the old days might have noticed that now she always kept her hands out of sight under the plaid rug.

One evening the aunt allowed herself to be persuaded to go with them. It was the first time she had set foot outside the house in a month and the air felt unnaturally heavy, for it was high summer and the scent of honeysuckle, mixed with the weedkiller the council had sprayed on the grass verges, made her head reel. Inside the mission hall the heat was overpowering. People fanned themselves with their gloves and hymn-sheets, and the aunt was surprised to see the number of souls who were prepared to brave such an evening under a baking tin roof. She sat next to a man who wheezed asthmatically, but she couldn't change places because every seat was taken. Cheryl's chair was right up at the front in the aisle, beside a sloping ramp that led up to the low platform. The aunt looked at the ramp but she had no inkling of what was about to happen; she was conscious only of the sweat seeking out and finding every crevice of her body under her clothes. Then the crowd – congregation didn't seem the right word, somehow, for such a collection of misfits – quickened in anticipation and Harold stepped into view to acknowledge their sudden excitement.

His face glowed even more painfully than she had ever

seen it, and he seemed to expand in size under the low corrugated roof. The aunt felt she was in danger of being suffocated by the emotion all about her; the man at her side had tears running down his face already, but before she could struggle from her seat, a hymn was being roared and she knew it was hopeless. Closing her eyes, she saw herself being borne out insensible, her heavy legs and underwear displayed for all this riff-raff to see. Then the singing ended and Harold's voice was ringing out above the 'Hallelujahs'.

'Oh, brothers and sisters, what a joy it is to see so many seekers after truth here tonight. How happy it makes me and, if I'm happy, the Lord is a million times more so. When I first began the good work here in this humble little hall, only a handful of believers came to hear the good news, only a handful, dear friends, but, since then the word has gone out, the word has multiplied, and look around you, just look and see for yourselves how the Bible message can never be denied or consigned to a dark and dusty corner. But, all this, dear friends, as you well know, has been due to someone here amongst us tonight, someone with a terrible shadow hanging over them because of an occasion of sin, a slip from God's good grace in a single unguarded moment. But allow our dear sister Cherith – oh, how sweet the name – to give her testimony, in her own words,' and, at that point, to the aunt's undiluted horror, two boys at the front rapidly wheeled the chair up the ramp and on to the platform.

The crowd seemed to hold its breath, only the flutter of hymn-sheets could be heard, and Harold Duff, with the proud smile of someone whose protegée is about to perform, stood there with a tambourine in his hand. Holding it aloft, he shook it once as some sort of signal, for the people vented breath in a deep collective sigh. The aunt couldn't take her eyes off her niece, her own blood on her brother's side, and she knew, oh, how well she knew, some hideous truth was about to be revealed about their life together. She saw the girl bring both hands out from under the rug she herself had bought for her, and, for a moment, look at them just in the way she used to. The gesture tugged

143

at the aunt's heart and she prayed, oh, if only the clock could be put back, but then the hands were raised in the air, shamelessly, it seemed to the woman suffering there in the heat, for all and sundry to admire and marvel over. The crowd sighed deeply and a smile broke out on the girl's face. It seemed to illuminate the dingy hall and everyone there, except the aunt, who, sensing her moment of shame had come at last, covered both ears with gloved hands. The smiling lips parted and the people settled themselves with pleasurable expectation to listen once more to the story they never tired of hearing.

'Dear sweet friends, these hands may look whiter than white to you, but once they dabbled in sin. Let me tell you how they led your sister astray and on to that downward path so that it may serve as a warning to you all. One afternoon, three friends and I set off innocently enough, with no thoughts in our heads...'